SOMETHING STINKS

The water roiled suddenly. Bubbles rose and burst, and following them came the shape of something foul, arching up out of the bayou. All the boys let out a common yell of alarm and scrambled backward on the nearby bank. They all managed to hang on to their fishing poles, despite their fear.

The shape in the water moved slowly toward shore. One of the boys, the tallest and oldest—who, because of those things, felt that he had to be the bravest as well—stepped forward tentatively. His eyes narrowed as he saw that the mysterious humpbacked shape was covered with some sort of cloth. A moment later, he realized it had to be a shirt.

"Hey! That be a man in th' water!"

DON'T MISS THESE
ALL-ACTION WESTERN SERIES
FROM THE BERKLEY PUBLISHING GROUP

THE GUNSMITH by J. R. Roberts
Clint Adams was a legend among lawmen, outlaws, and ladies. They called him . . . the Gunsmith.

LONGARM by Tabor Evans
The popular long-running series about U.S. Deputy Marshal Long—his life, his loves, his fight for justice.

SLOCUM by Jake Logan
Today's longest-running action Western. John Slocum rides a deadly trail of hot blood and cold steel.

BUSHWHACKERS by B. J. Lanagan
An all-new series by the creators of Longarm! The rousing adventures of the most brutal gang of cutthroats ever assembled—Quantrill's Raiders.

TABOR EVANS

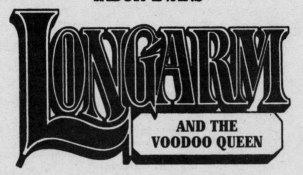

LONGARM

AND THE VOODOO QUEEN

J

JOVE BOOKS, NEW YORK

LONGARM AND THE VOODOO QUEEN

A Jove Book / published by arrangement with
the author

PRINTING HISTORY
Jove edition / December 1997

The Putnam Berkley World Wide Web site address is
http://www.berkley.com

ISBN: 0-515-12191-6

A JOVE BOOK®
Jove Books are published by The Berkley Publishing Group,
a member of Penguin Putnam Inc.,
200 Madison Avenue, New York, New York 10016.
JOVE and the "J" design are trademarks
belonging to Jove Publications, Inc.

PRINTED IN THE UNITED STATES OF AMERICA

10 9 8 7 6 5 4 3 2 1

AND THE
VOODOO QUEEN

Chapter 1

The sun was just peeking over the moss-draped cypresses when the children came running along the bank of the bayou, laughing and capering, waving the bamboo poles they clutched in their hands. They came to a stop at their favorite fishing spot. Hands were plunged into the wooden bucket full of chopped mullet, and the slimy little bits of dead sea creatures were carefully impaled on bent pins that served as hooks. Here under the trees, the air was already hot and still despite the early hour, and the surface of the bayou lay flat and silent, broken only by an occasional ring of concentric ripples caused by insects landing on the water and then taking off again. The soft, liquid voices of the boys were the only sounds.

Hooks baited, they cast out into the water, and the bent pins made more ripples as they struck the placid surface. The ripples ran outward from the points of impact and gradually died away. The boys fell silent, content in their companionship and in this time and place.

The water roiled suddenly. Bubbles rose and burst, and following them came the humped shape of something foul, arching up out of the bayou. All the boys let out a common yell of alarm and scrambled backward on the nearby bank. They all managed to hang on to their fishing poles, despite their fear.

The shape in the water moved slowly toward shore. One of the boys, the tallest and oldest—who, because of those things, felt that he had to be the bravest as well—stepped forward tentatively. His eyes narrowed as he saw that the mysterious humpbacked shape was covered with some sort of cloth. A moment later, he realized it had to be a shirt.

"Hey! That be a man in th' water!"

Now the boys clustered closer to the edge of the bayou. Part of the mystery had been explained. Young as they were, all of them had seen death before. It was a part of everyday life for those who lived on and around the waters of the great river and the gulf into which it flowed. They were Delta boys, and they knew death, all right, and feared it only slightly.

The oldest and tallest boy pulled his line from the water and cast out toward the floating shape. It took him a couple of tries, but then he hooked the shirt. "He'p me pull 'im in," he told his friends, and eager hands reached for the line. "Careful, careful," he cautioned. "This here line, he ain't gon' hold too much weight."

Slowly, they hauled the floating thing toward the shore. A few moments later, it bumped against the bank, and the tallest, oldest boy said, "Hold 'im there. Maurice, Richard, you gimme a hand."

The three of them reached down and caught hold of the waterlogged shirt and pulled. An arm broke from the water and flopped onto the bank. The hand at the end of that arm was as white and pale as the belly of a gar. The flesh had been gnawed in places by small fish.

The boys pulled harder and the man's head came out of the water, his long, lank hair streaming water as it fell over the empty holes where his eyes had been. All the boys felt a fresh surge of fear as they saw the tattered, incomplete face of the dead man. But they kept pulling, the weight of the body heavy from all the water it had absorbed, and the other arm came out, and the torso down to the waist, and then the boys fell backward on the bank because that was all that was left of the man and there was nothing to hold him in the water. They let go of him and scrambled away, and all of them looked in horror at the ragged place where the corpse ended, and knew that more than likely a gator had chomped the man plumb in two.

Released of their hold, the half of the dead man that they had pulled from the bayou rolled from its side onto its back in a ghastly semblance of life. A shaft of sunlight, green-tinged from the thick vegetation through which it filtered, struck the chest of the dead man and reflected dully from the bit of tarnished metal that was pinned there. The tallest, oldest boy saw the reflection and edged closer to take a look, the need to be the leader once again overcoming his fear. He put his hands on his bony knees, bare beneath the cut-off trousers that were his only garment, and his lips moved a little as he read the words engraved on the piece of metal. He'd had enough schooling so that he could make some sense of them, though he had no idea why such a man—or at least, *part* of such a man—had been floating in the bayou.

The dead man was wearing the badge of a United States deputy marshal.

Chapter 2

"You a superstitious man, Custis?" asked Billy Vail as he dropped a thin sheaf of papers on his desk.

Longarm cocked his right ankle on his left knee and leaned back in the leather chair in front of Vail's desk. He took a puff on the cheroot he had just lit and then said, "Not so's you'd notice, I don't reckon."

The chief marshal, whose pink face and balding pate made him appear deceptively cherubic, said, "Black cats don't scare you when they cross your path?"

Longarm frowned, wondering what in tarnation Vail was getting at. "I ain't overly fond of the critters," he said, "but I don't run home and stay in bed for the rest of the day whenever I see one. Leastways not alone." He grinned, but Vail didn't seem to notice.

"Good, because I'm sending you to New Orleans."

Longarm didn't see what that had to do with superstition. True, there were parts of Louisiana that could be downright spooky: the swamps and the bayous and those mossy old plantation houses that had been abandoned to rot with only ghostly memories left to inhabit them. Longarm had never

4

considered himself an overly imaginative man, but as he thought of such places, he had to admit that a tiny shiver went through him deep inside. But he had been to Louisiana and New Orleans itself many times, and he certainly didn't feel nervous about going there again.

"That's a little out of our usual territory, ain't it?"

"That's why you're going," said Vail. "I know some of your cases have taken you to New Orleans in the past, but you're not well known there, by any means. You wouldn't be as likely to be recognized as you would be in, say, Cheyenne or Deadwood."

Longarm inclined his head slightly in acknowledgment of his boss's point. "I reckon that's right."

"We got a request from the U.S. marshal's office in New Orleans—"

"For somebody to work on a case incognito, as they say," Longarm concluded for Vail.

"That's right." Vail shoved the stack of papers across the desk toward Longarm. "Take a look at these reports, Custis."

Longarm leaned forward and picked up the documents, then began reading them quickly. He was long since accustomed to scanning official reports like these and picking out the essential elements in them, so that he could mentally digest the important information without wasting any time. In this case, he saw right away that the reports concerned the murder of a U.S. deputy marshal named Douglas Ramsey.

Longarm's eyes narrowed as he read how Ramsey's body had been pulled from a bayou by some boys who had been out fishing before making their grisly discovery. *Half* of Ramsey's body had been pulled from the bayou, Longarm realized as he read further. That was all that had been left. The rest of the lawman had undoubtedly wound up as alligator bait.

"Damn," breathed Longarm. "That's one hell of a way to go."

"Ramsey didn't die from the alligator attack," said Vail,

5

not needing to ask which part of the report had prompted Longarm's comment. ''The coroner down there established that he had been murdered. He had a knife wound in his back, and he was dead before he ever went into the water. Feeding him to the gators was just the killer's way of disposing of the body.''

''But it didn't work,'' Longarm pointed out.

''Nope. For some reason, part of the body was left in the water, and when it filled up with enough gas, it bobbed to the surface just in time to scare a couple of years' growth out of those boys who found it.''

Longarm paged through the reports. ''According to this, Ramsey was working on a smuggling case. There's always been a heap of smuggling all over that Mississippi Delta. What was important enough about this one to start a federal deputy poking around?''

Vail grimaced as he said, ''Politics. You know how corrupt the city government of New Orleans has always been— before the war, during the war, during Reconstruction. And now, a few years after the Reconstructionists were chased out, everything's still just about the same. Only the names and the faces change, and the graft goes on. That's led to a strong reform movement in the city. It never really seems to accomplish much, mind you, except to swap one set of rascals for another, but it's there anyway.''

Longarm nodded, even though he wasn't sure where this conversation was going. Vail wasn't really telling him anything he didn't already know.

''One of the reformers managed to get himself appointed as a special prosecutor, and he petitioned the federal government asking for help in cleaning things up. One of the groups he's been going after are the smugglers. The legitimate merchants in New Orleans have always been frustrated because it's easier to buy just about anything from the smugglers, rather than through legal channels.''

''So the deputy marshal who wound up in the bayou, this fella Ramsey, he was working for the special prosecutor?''

Vail nodded. "That's right."

"And that's what you want me to do," Longarm said, his voice flat.

"The difference is, nobody in New Orleans knows you, like I said before. You'll be able to find out who's behind the smuggling by working in amongst the people who are carrying it out."

Longarm sighed, unsure what to tell Vail. He had never turned down an assignment outright, and he didn't want to start now. He had a reputation, whether justified or not, for being able to handle the tough cases. Longarm figured he was good at his job. He wasn't given to false modesty. But he knew as well how often luck had been on his side, and from everything he had read in those reports and everything Billy Vail had told him, this case was going to require an extra amount of good fortune.

To gain himself a little extra time to think about it, Longarm said, "I still don't understand why you asked me if I was superstitious, Billy. I reckon Ramsey ran into some bad luck and all, what with being knifed and then half-eaten by a gator, but that was just the doing of the crooks he was trying to chase down."

"I suppose so," Vail said heavily, "but there's one thing that's not in those reports, Custis. The chief marshal in the New Orleans office wired me personally about it when he asked for the loan of my best man. Ramsey's body was found day before yesterday. Yesterday morning, something else turned up on the doorstep of the marshal's office."

Vail looked down at the desk, and Longarm waited in silence for him to go on.

"It was a little cloth doll," Vail said when he finally looked up again. "It was made to look sort of like Ramsey, right down to the badge pinned on his chest. And it was cut in half, Custis. The bottom half was nowhere to be found."

Well, thought Longarm a few days later as he stepped onto the wharf where the riverboat *Dixie Belle* had tied up, nobody had ever accused him of being overly smart. Some men would have refused this job, even if it had meant turning in their badges. Not him. He had come to the Crescent City to take over the case that had gotten the last man not only killed but also hexed somehow. That crude doll left at the chief marshal's office had been an unmistakable warning. Some kind of evil voodoo magic was at work in New Orleans.

Or at least that was what somebody wanted the authorities to believe. As Longarm had told Billy Vail, he wasn't a superstitious man. He was much more worried about a knife in the back or a hidden gunman than he was about witchcraft.

From Denver he had taken a train to St. Louis, and there boarded the riverboat that had brought him down the Mississippi. Now, as he stepped off the boat, a hot, humid wind hit him in the face. He frowned. As accustomed as he was to the high, dry air of Colorado, it always took him a while to adjust every time a case brought him to the Gulf Coast. He recalled a couple of jobs that had taken him to the Corpus Christi area, over in Texas. Pretty country once you got used to it, but the weather sure made a man sweat.

Longarm ignored the sultry heat as much as he could. Instead of his usual snuff-brown Stetson, he wore a cream-colored planter's hat, and a lightweight suit of the same color in place of his customary brown tweeds. He still wore a vest, though, a silk vest with fancy gold embroidery. His watch chain stretched across the vest, the heavy gold turnip in the left-hand pocket, the wicked little .44 derringer that was attached to the other end of the chain in his right-hand pocket, as usual. The string tie he wore around his neck was a little wider, a little more flamboyant than the one he normally sported. His Winchester and saddle had been left behind in his Denver rooming house for this trip, but the cross-draw rig in which he carried his Colt was belted around his lean waist as usual. Longarm thought he looked like a damn riverboat gambler, and he felt a little seedy and shady.

Which was good, because that was precisely what he was supposed to look like. Nobody was going to mistake him for a lawman in this getup, and he wasn't carrying his badge or his other bona fides either. If he got into any trouble that he couldn't handle himself, he was supposed to seek out that special prosecutor who had requested Uncle Sam's help and use the phrase "Pikes Peak." That would identify him as a federal man.

Longarm had snorted in disgust when Henry, Billy Vail's clerk, had filled him in on these clandestine arrangements. Plenty of times in the past, Longarm had worked incognito, but this was carrying things to a ridiculous extreme.

Still, the more he'd thought about it on the trip to New Orleans, the more he'd figured the precautions just might save his life. The whole thing was squarely in his hands. He had to depend on his own wits to survive and find out the things he needed to know. He was willing to run that risk.

The only baggage he had was the carpetbag that dangled from his left hand. He raised his right hand to hail one of the hacks that had swarmed to the docks for the arrival of the *Dixie Belle*. One of the carriages drew up beside him, and Longarm stepped up into it, saying to the driver, "The St. Charles Hotel." With a grin, the driver flicked his reins and got the horse moving once more. The St. Charles was the best hotel in the city, and most passengers bound for it could be counted on for a generous tip on top of the fare.

Longarm settled back to enjoy the ride. As always, New Orleans was busy, its cobblestone streets thronged with people and horses and carriages and wagons. The buildings were a blend of the very old and the very new, their architecture a dizzying array of Spanish, French, and American influences. The hack carrying Longarm passed square stone buildings devoid of any personality; they could have been in any city in the country. But next to them were old mansions fronted by white columns dripping with moss, and across the street might be a Spanish palace like an illustration from *The Alhambra*. Longarm grinned and lit a cheroot. You never knew what you were going to see next in New Orleans.

And that was especially true at this time of year, he

9

thought. Carnival was well under way, with Fat Tuesday—Mardi Gras—fast approaching. Masked, costumed figures pranced among the businessmen and housewives moving along the streets, even at this midday hour. A Harlequin with painted face caught Longarm's eye and waved madly at him as the hack went by. Solemnly, Longarm lifted a hand and touched a finger to the brim of his hat in salute. The Harlequin clasped his hands under his chin and looked devoutly thankful to have been acknowledged.

Longarm shook his head. These folks down here knew how to have a good time, all right, but he thought they sometimes got a mite carried away.

A few minutes later, the hack pulled up in front of the St. Charles. If Longarm remembered right, this was at least the third incarnation of the hotel. After being built in the 1830s, the St. Charles had burned down and been replaced twice. It was a massive, opulent building that took up an entire city block and was surrounded by columns that supported a balcony with an elaborate wrought-iron railing on the second floor. Marble steps led up to the entrance, and a doorman in a uniform that would have been more suited to a naval commodore sprang down those steps to be waiting as Longarm disembarked from the hack.

Taking a five-dollar gold piece from his pocket, Longarm flipped the coin to the hack driver, who plucked it deftly from midair as it spun toward him. "Thank you, suh," the driver said with a broad grin. The tip was extravagant, but that was just the sort of man Longarm wanted people to think he was.

The doorman reached for Longarm's carpetbag. "Take that for you, suh?" he asked.

Longarm shook his head. "No, thanks, I'll manage it myself."

The doorman looked crestfallen and said, "As you wish, suh," but he brightened up when Longarm pressed a gold piece into his hand.

10

"May be needing some help later, though," said Longarm, and the doorman nodded eagerly.

"Anythin' you want, suh, you jus' let me know."

Longarm went up the steps and into the hotel as more of the Carnival revelers came along the street behind him, tooting horns. The noise faded as soon as he was in the huge, marble-floored lobby of the St. Charles. Instead, a quiet hush prevailed among the potted palms, a silence that sounded somehow like money.

The desk clerk was a thin-faced man with slicked-back hair. He looked at Longarm expectantly, and Longarm said, "I wired for a reservation. Name's Parker." He was using his middle name as an alias, as he sometimes did when he was keeping his real identity hidden.

"Yes, Mr. Parker, of course," said the clerk. "We've been holding the room." He turned the register around and slid it across the highly polished counter toward Longarm. "If you'd just sign in . . ."

Longarm scrawled *C. Parker, St. Louis* in the space the clerk indicated. The man turned the book back toward him and went on. "How long will you be staying with us, sir?"

"I'm not sure," said Longarm. "Several days anyway."

"Very well. You'll be in Room 312."

The clerk was reaching for a room key on the board behind him when a hand fell softly on Longarm's sleeve and a husky voice said, "You are a very lucky man, *m'sieu*."

Longarm looked over at the woman who had spoken to him, and saw that she had a black domino mask surrounded by precious stones held in front of her eyes.

That didn't make much difference. He didn't have to see her face to know that she was one of the most beautiful women he had encountered in a long time.

Chapter 3

"I certainly am a lucky man," Longarm murmured as he looked at the woman. "Fortunate because I've just made your acquaintance, have I not, my dear?"

"*Qui.*" She held out a hand with slender, graceful fingers, and he took it and bent over it to brush his lips lightly against the back of it. "I am Annie Clement," she said.

"Custis Parker," he told her. "From St. Louis. And I'm very glad I decided to come down here to New Orleans."

She was tall and slender, though curved in all the right places, as the expensive gown she wore displayed enticingly. Most of the deeply tanned valley between her breasts was visible, and Longarm gazed openly at her charms. She had thick, honey-colored hair that fell in waves to her shoulders, and her eyes behind the mask were an intriguing green with light-colored flecks in them, reminding Longarm of foam on an open sea. Her lips were full and red and curved in a smile as she slowly lowered the mask so that Longarm could appreciate the full impact of her beauty.

From the corner of his eye, Longarm saw the hotel clerk lean forward. "Can I help you, Miss Clement?" the clerk asked. Obviously, this lovely young woman was known to him.

Annie turned her head and smiled at the man. "No, thank you, Jack. This gentleman has already introduced himself to me." She linked her arm with Longarm's. "And now he's going to take me into the salon and buy me a drink."

"I'd like that just fine," Longarm told her, "but there's just one thing I need to get cleared up first. By any chance are you a, ah, working girl, Miss Clement?"

Annie laughed lightly at the question, but the desk clerk's eyebrows shot up as he looked scandalized. "Mr. Parker," he said sternly, "the St. Charles does not allow—"

"It's all right, Jack," said Annie. "M'sieu Parker is a guest in New Orleans and cannot be expected to know everything about our fair city." To Longarm, she said, "No, I'm not a soiled dove, M'sieu Parker, if that's what you thought."

"Not really," said Longarm, "but I like to make sure how deep the water is before I go diving in headfirst."

"Around here you'll find that the waters are seldom deep . . . but they can still be treacherous." She steered him toward the arched entrance of the salon. "Now come along with me. Put yourself in my hands."

"That's a mighty appealing prospect," said Longarm, and the comment drew another laugh from her.

Behind them, the desk clerk called out, "I'll have your bag taken up to your room, Mr. Parker."

A waiter in the salon, who clearly knew who Annie was just as the desk clerk had, showed them to a table that was given at least an illusion of privacy by the potted plants that screened it off from the rest of the room. Longarm felt a little as if he had somehow wound up in a jungle. He leaned across the table toward Annie and asked, "What would you like to drink?"

"Wine would be nice."

Longarm repeated the order to the hovering waiter, then added, "Maryland rye for me, Tom Moore if you've got it."

"Indeed we do, sir," said the waiter. "I'll be right back."

While they waited for the drinks, Annie clasped her hands together in front of her on the table and looked over them at Longarm. "And what brings you to New Orleans, M'sieu Parker? Business . . . or pleasure?"

"Ten minutes ago, I would have said business," replied Longarm, "but that was before I met you, ma'am. Now I would have to say that I'm hoping for a combination of the two."

"How gallant of you. What line of business are you in?"

"Importing and exporting," said Longarm, trying to convey with his tone of voice that even though she was a beautiful woman, he wasn't quite ready to reveal all of his secrets to her just yet.

"How interesting. My brother and I export sugar to your country."

Longarm frowned slightly. "I figured that you lived here in New Orleans. Folks seem to know you pretty well in these parts."

"Oh, we have a house here," she said. "The Clement mansion, on Chartres Street, not far from here. It has been in the family for over a hundred years. But our real home is on Saint Laurent."

Longarm shook his head and said, "Don't reckon I've heard of it."

"It is a small island in the West Indies, where our sugar plantation is located. Paul and I travel here several times each year." A smile lit up Annie's face. "Like you, M'sieu Parker, we attempt to combine business with pleasure."

"A mighty sensible approach," said Longarm. "Here come our drinks."

The waiter placed a glass of wine in front of Annie, then gave Longarm a shot of Maryland rye along with a tumbler of water to chase it. Then the waiter withdrew diffidently, and once again Longarm and Annie had at least the semblance of being alone.

They clinked their glasses together, and Annie said, "To

New Orleans . . . and all the possibilities it holds.''

"To New Orleans," agreed Longarm. He tossed back the rye, savoring its rich, smoky taste. So far, his trip to the Crescent City had been quite pleasurable.

But no matter what he had told Annie Clement, he was really here for one reason and one reason alone: to find whoever was responsible for the murder of Douglas Ramsey and bring the killer, or killers, to justice.

Annie sipped her wine and then said, "I shall have to introduce you to my brother. I'm sure you and Paul would have much in common."

Longarm wasn't so certain of that, and while this momentary dalliance with Annie had been enjoyable, he didn't want to waste his time meeting some wastrel son of an old, wealthy French family, which was clearly what the Clements were. Still, he didn't want to insult Annie, so he said noncommittally, "That would be nice, but we'll have to see how things work out."

"*I* know," she said, brightening even more with the idea that had come to her. "Why don't you come out with us tonight? We are going to dine and then visit a place we know on Gallatin Street where we can gamble. Perhaps you have heard of it—the Brass Pelican?"

Longarm was starting to shake his head when Annie added, "It is owned by a man named Millard, Jasper Millard."

Longarm hoped he was able to conceal his surprise. He had heard of Jasper Millard, all right, but certainly not for the same reason that Annie knew the man. Millard's name had been in those reports Longarm had read in Billy Vail's office back in Denver. He was one of the men suspected by the special prosecutor of being involved in the smuggling that was so widespread in the Mississippi Delta.

Longarm had considered using Millard to pick up the trail of Ramsey's murderer. Now, through happenstance, he had a perfect way into Millard's gambling club, and he would be a fool to pass it up.

Or was it happenstance? he asked himself abruptly, still controlling the expression on his face as thoughts raced through his head with lightning-fast speed. Was he being set up somehow? Were the smugglers already on to him, already aware of his true identity? Maybe Annie Clement was just the lovely bait in a deadly trap. . . .

But Longarm didn't think so. He couldn't see how it was possible for any of the criminal element in New Orleans to know who he really was. He had bought his own ticket on the *Dixie Belle* in St. Louis and paid cash for it, and he'd had no contact with the authorities while he was there. As far as anyone on the riverboat knew, he was exactly what he appeared to be, a businessman, just a little bit disreputable, on his way to New Orleans. And during the hour or so that he had been here in the Crescent City, he was certain he hadn't done anything to give himself away.

Nope, he thought, this was purely a case of serendipity, enjoying the two-bit word he had picked up in his reading at the Denver Public Library near the end of each month when his money was low and his next paycheck was still a few days away.

"That's mighty kind of you," he said to Annie, "and I'll sure take you up on the invitation. If you're certain your brother won't mind, that is."

"Paul will not mind." She rolled her eyes a little. "There is nothing he enjoys more than discussing business, so you will have to promise me, M'sieu Parker, that you will not allow him to monopolize your time all evening. There is dancing as well as gambling at the Brass Pelican, and you must dance with me while we are there."

"I'm looking forward to it," Longarm said, and meant it.

Annie stood up, and Longarm got hurriedly to his feet to help her with her chair. "We will pick you up in our carriage at seven o'clock," she said.

"I'll be ready," he promised.

"Until then, M'sieu Parker . . . *adieu*."

Longarm watched her walk away, and he wasn't the only

one. Every man in the salon was admiring the graceful sway of her hips. Longarm didn't allow himself to feel any jealousy; he hadn't known her long enough, or well enough, for that.

But he had a hunch that before his trip to New Orleans was over, he was going to.

Longarm went back to the desk to pick up his room key, and while he was there he asked the clerk to have all the local newspapers sent up to his room. The man nodded and said, "Yes, sir, Mr. Parker, I'll take care of that right away." They were eager to please here in New Orleans, thought Longarm as he went upstairs. A purple-jacketed bellboy arrived with the stack of papers a few minutes after Longarm had let himself into Room 312 and found it to be as comfortably appointed as he had expected.

It was also empty, no hidden gunmen lurking there waiting to murder him. Longarm wasn't really anticipating any trouble this soon, but it never hurt to be careful.

He spent an hour or so reading through the newspapers, familiarizing himself with what was going on in New Orleans at the present time. As Billy Vail had told him and the reports had verified, there was a strong reform movement under way, its aim to clean up the corruption in city government and shut down the Louisiana State Lottery, which was also riddled with graft and bribery. The lottery, and the men behind it, had so much power that the entire system was referred to by editorialists in antilottery papers as "the Golden Octopus." That situation was interesting, but it wasn't what had brought Longarm to New Orleans. He concentrated instead on stories relating to the smuggling, which seemed as widespread as the lottery. He found several stories which mentioned the special prosecutor whose cries for help had brought him here. The man promised in no uncertain terms that the smuggling rings would be broken up and their hold on the Delta country smashed. Longarm snorted as he read the inflammatory quotes. That was just like a politician, he thought, to stir up a mess and then leave it for somebody else to clean up.

He put the papers aside and went downstairs for a late lunch in the hotel dining room, then returned to his room and slept for several hours. It was likely to be a late night coming up, and Longarm wanted to be well rested.

He changed his shirt, but was wearing the same suit and hat when he came down to the hotel lobby a little before seven o'clock. There was no sign of Annie Clement or her brother yet, so Longarm wandered over to the desk, where the same clerk was still on duty. Longarm had tipped the man handsomely when he asked for the newspapers to be sent up, so he thought it was probably safe to ask a question or two.

"You seem to know Miss Clement pretty well," he said to the clerk, as if he was only making idle talk while waiting. "I'm supposed to dine with her and her brother tonight."

"I'm sure you'll enjoy yourself, Mr. Parker. They're a charming couple." The clerk allowed himself the faintest lift of an eyebrow. "And Miss Clement is undeniably one of the most beautiful women in New Orleans—which is saying a great deal indeed."

"You won't get any argument from me on either of those points, friend," Longarm assured him. "What's her brother like?"

The clerk's tone dropped a little and took on a conspiratorial edge. "Well . . . he's a man with a certain reputation. . . ."

"As a businessman, you mean," said Longarm, playing dumb. "Miss Clement told me they were sugar exporters."

"Yessss . . . but I had more in mind Mr. Clement's reputation as a gambler. *And* something of a ladies' man."

Longarm grinned, stuck an unlit cheroot in his mouth, and said around it, "So he likes the cards and the ladies, eh?"

"So it's said, sir. I wouldn't really know."

I'll just bet you wouldn't, thought Longarm. Hotel clerks saw the best and the worst of folks, and they generally knew

18

the truth of the matter about as well as anyone this side of the local law—and sometimes better.

"Wonder what Miss Clement was doing here earlier today," Longarm mused aloud. "She said she and her brother have a house here in town."

"Oh, she comes here often," said the clerk, "to have a drink or to dine with us or simply to visit friends that might be stopping here."

Longarm grinned again. "So it was just good fortune that she and I met. Hope that luck stays with me. Miss Clement promised they'd take me to a gambling club called the Brass Pelican. Said it was over on Gallatin Street."

The clerk's eyes widened slightly, and Longarm saw that his shot in the dark had hit something. "You should be careful over there, Mr. Parker," cautioned the clerk. "The Brass Pelican is known for its rather, ah, notorious clientele. All of the establishments on Gallatin Street are sometimes frequented by, ah, undesirables."

That didn't come as any surprise to Longarm since Jasper Millard, the owner of the place, was known to have connections with the smuggling rings that operated along the bayous. He said, "I can take care of myself . . . and some folks have sort of figured I'm a mite notorious and undesirable myself."

He chuckled, and the clerk joined in uneasily. Longarm wanted to be known as someone who might skirt the law on occasion, and he figured he had just reinforced that image in the clerk's mind. Now, if the right people believed the same thing about him, he might be on his way to discovering what he had come to New Orleans to find out.

At that moment, the doors of the hotel opened and Annie Clement came in, followed by a tall, thin man in evening clothes, a cape, and a top hat. Annie was gorgeous in a shimmery, dark gray gown trimmed with white fur, and her face lit up with a smile as she saw Longarm. She held out both hands as she came toward him, and he took them and squeezed warmly.

19

"M'sieu Parker, how wonderful to see you again," she said. "I want you to meet my brother. Paul, this is M'sieu Parker, who is visiting New Orleans from St. Louis."

"Custis Parker," Longarm said, introducing himself as he shook hands with Paul Clement.

The Frenchman had a dark, narrow face that seemed to fall naturally into sardonic, half-amused lines. He was clean-shaven and had dark, curly hair under the top hat. "I am pleased to make your acquaintance, M'sieu Parker," he said. "My dear sister has told me so much about you, I find it difficult to believe that the two of you met only today."

"It's the truth," said Longarm. "Miss Annie here was the first one to really welcome me to New Orleans. I'm grateful to her for making me feel at home—and for inviting me along with the two of you tonight. I hope I'm not being an imposition."

Clement waved a hand languidly. "Of course not! We're perfectly happy to have you accompany us. As I believe Annie told you, we don't actually live here in the city either, so I suppose we're all visitors in New Orleans." He added, "We know it quite well, though."

"I'm glad of that," Longarm told him. "I'm relying on the two of you to be my guides."

"Come along, then, Custis," Annie said, calling him by his given name for the first time as she linked her arm with his. "The night is young, but there is much to see and do."

The three of them went out of the hotel. An elegant black carriage waited at the curb. It had gilt trim and a couple of oil lamps attached to its roof, and six fine black horses were hitched to it. A driver in fancy livery handled the team from the high seat in the front of the vehicle. This was a far cry from some of the mud wagons and Concord stagecoaches he had ridden out West, thought Longarm. For the time being, he was really living high on the hog.

Paul Clement opened the carriage door for his sister, then stood back and gestured for Longarm to board next. Annie patted the upholstered bench next to her. Longarm hesitated

20

for a second, then took the seat. Clement climbed in and settled himself on the opposite bench, so that he would be riding facing backward. He didn't seem to mind.

As the carriage began rolling through the streets of New Orleans, Clement said, "Darling Annie tells me you are an importer and exporter, M'sieu Parker."

"I dabble in a little of this and a little of that," Longarm said vaguely. "To tell you the truth, I'm sort of between enterprises right now. I was told that this was a good town for a man wanting to make a fresh start."

"True, there are boundless opportunities ... if a man knows what he wants and is prepared to do whatever is necessary in order to obtain it."

It was shadowy inside the carriage, but Longarm had a feeling Clement was watching him closely. He said coolly, "I've always had a pretty good idea where the road was leading me."

"All roads ultimately lead to the same place, do they not? I speak, of course, of the grave."

Annie said, "That's enough, Paul. I made M'sieu Parker promise that you and he would not spend the entire evening talking business, and I will not allow your morbid philosophy to take over either." She slipped her hand inside Longarm's and leaned closer to him. "I think you will like the restaurant we have selected, Custis. It has the finest food in New Orleans."

"Sounds good," said Longarm, and he hoped it would be. But he doubted seriously if whatever the restaurant had to offer could compete with biscuits and son-of-a-bitch stew and a cup of Arbuckle's on a clear night in the high country under the western stars.

The restaurant was an unprepossessing place on St. Louis Street called Antoine's. As the carriage pulled up in front and Longarm, Annie, and Clement got out, Longarm smelled some of the most enticing aromas he had ever encountered floating out the open windows of the building. Inside, the dining room was rather plainly furnished, but the delicious smells were even stronger. The place was busy too, but Longarm and his companions were immediately shown to one of the few empty tables. Moments later, bowls of steaming soup were brought to them, as if they had been expected—as indeed they had been, Clement confirmed a few moments later. "Annie and I always dine here at least once whenever we are in New Orleans," he added.

Longarm could understand why. The soup, which had bits of crawfish floating in it, was rich and thick and savory. It was followed by tender veal in sauce, steamed vegetables, and loaves of French bread dripping in melted butter. The bread was crispy on the outside, soft on the inside, and steam rose from it when Longarm took his first bite. He had to admit that everything was good, and he ate heartily. So did Annie and her brother. Longarm found himself watching Annie approvingly. He liked a woman with a good appetite. Everything was washed down with excellent wines, first white, then red, and by the time the meal was over, Longarm was feeling pleasantly stuffed.

He stifled a groan as he stood up to leave with Annie and Clement. Both of them had packed away as much food and drink as he had, but neither seemed to be feeling any ill effects. Longarm could have used a nap.

He came fully awake as they got back into the carriage and headed for Gallatin Street, however. No longer was he indulging himself, although he seemed as relaxed as ever. Now he was working again, and inside, every nerve was alert.

The carriage turned from St. Louis Street onto Decatur and headed along the river, past the Pontalba Apartment Buildings with their luxurious accommodations, past Jackson Square with its memorial statue of Old Hickory, and along the rear of the old French Market before jogging to the right into Gallatin Street itself.

Longarm had seen places like it before: Front Street in Abilene during the days of Wild Bill Hickok, Allen Street in Tombstone, Ferguson Street in Cheyenne. It was an area of saloons, gambling dens, whorehouses, dance halls, pawn-shops, and seedy offices used by businessmen who were no more honest than they had to be. Women in frilly night-clothes leaned over the balcony railings of the buildings the carriage passed, calling to potential customers on the street below. Men stood on corners, hawking goods that were un-doubtedly stolen. Dark-mouthed alleys opened frequently from the street, and the noises that came from them gave ample warning that it would not be wise to venture down them alone. Longarm glanced in one window as they passed and saw a redheaded woman standing there nude, her lush body on display in the light of a lantern that hung above her head. Her breasts were large, the nipples rouged, and one hand was between her legs as she caressed herself. Annie was looking in the same direction, but if she saw the lewd spectacle, she gave no sign of it.

"Ah, here we are," Clement announced a few moments later. "The Brass Pelican."

The outside of the gambling club appeared to be better kept up than many of the buildings in the area. It was a low brick structure with a pair of whitewashed columns flanking the heavy entrance door. Above the door, mounted on an iron rod that protruded from the building, was the statue that gave the club its name. Longarm had to admit that the sculpture was an accurate rendering of a pelican. The bird's wings were lifted, as if it was ready to take off, but its long legs were still curled underneath its body. The huge beak was pointed down at the short flagstone walk leading to the en-trance, and the pelican appeared to be casting a skeptical eye at the patrons who passed back and forth beneath it.

Clement stepped down from the carriage first, followed by Longarm. Longarm hesitated, unsure whether or not he should offer his hand to Annie or allow her brother to assist her down. She held out both hands as she stepped through the carriage door, however, so both Longarm and Clement had one to grasp. She linked arms with them and walked between them up to the door of the Brass Pelican.

23

A huge black man wearing a uniform similar to that of the doorman at the St. Charles Hotel was on duty there. He greeted the newcomers with a broad smile and said, "Good evenin', Mr. Clement, suh. And to you as well, ma'am."

"Good evening, Luther," replied Clement. "This is Mr. Parker. He's our guest for the evening."

"Yes, suh." The doorman nodded respectfully to Longarm. "How do, Mr. Parker."

Longarm returned the man's nod, then walked into the club with Annie and her brother as Luther opened the door. The sound of someone playing a piano quite loudly came to Longarm's ears, which was no surprise. Just about every saloon and gambling joint in the world had a piano player, no matter where it was. In this case, though, the fella pounding on the ivories actually seemed to have some musical talent, and the piano itself was almost in tune. That was pretty rare.

The air was thick with noise. The music, the laughter of women, the clatter of the roulette wheel and the rattle of dice, the almost prayerful words of the gamblers as they called on this spin of the wheel or this throw of the dice to come out in their favor for a change, the exultant shouts and the bitter curses when the outcome of the play was determined . . . it was all familiar to Longarm. He had heard it in a hundred saloons, in a hundred different towns. And the smells were the same too. Tobacco, whiskey, spilled beer, cheap perfume, unwashed human flesh. Not really a pleasant odor, but one to which a man could become accustomed, and a part of him would miss it all, the noise and the stink both, whenever he found himself in a place that was quiet and clean and well lighted.

Longarm put a cheroot in his mouth and clamped his teeth down on it. A place like this always made him feel as if he had just come home.

Most of the big main room was taken up with gambling tables and apparatus, he saw as he looked around. But there was a tiny dance floor, as Annie had mentioned earlier in the day, tucked away in the left rear corner. A mahogany bar ran down the right-hand side of the room, and at the end of it was a door that no doubt led into some back rooms where other business was conducted.

Standing at the end of the bar near the door was a tall, burly man whose head was as hairless as a billiard ball. He wasn't old, however. Longarm judged the man's age to be about the same as his own. He wore a dark, conservative suit that might have belonged to a banker or a lawyer instead of a saloonkeeper and proprietor of a gambling den. He chewed on a long, fat cigar and toyed with an empty shot glass as his eyes surveyed the place, constantly on the move. Longarm didn't have to be told who he was. The bald man's attitude alone was enough for Longarm to peg him as Jasper Millard.

Sure enough, as soon as he had checked his hat and cape, Paul Clement headed straight for the bald man, leaving Longarm and Annie to follow him across the crowded room. Clement raised a hand in greeting, and even over the clamor, Longarm heard him say, "Good evening, Jasper! Busy night tonight."

"Always," grunted Millard as Longarm and Annie came up to join him and Clement. "The Good Lord willing, it'll stay that way." He looked at Longarm with shrewd, dark eyes. "Who's your new friend?"

Longarm stuck out his hand, and without waiting for Clement to introduce him, he said, "Name's Custis Parker, down from St. Louis to do a little business."

Millard took Longarm's hand in a bone-crushing grip. Longarm gave as good as he got and saw a flicker of respect in Millard's eyes. "Just exactly what line of work are you in, Mr. Parker?" asked Millard.

"Just exactly whatever'll make me the most money," said Longarm with a grin. "That's the best kind of business, don't you think?"

"Damn right." Millard angled his bald head toward the bar. "Have a drink on me, Parker. And you two as well, of course, Clement."

Longarm was doubtful that Annie would be able to get a glass of wine here in this rough-and-tumble spot, but the bartender surprised him, holding out the delicate crystal glass to her without even being told what the lady wanted to drink. Clearly, this wasn't her first visit to the Brass Pelican either. Clement asked for bourbon, while Longarm ordered Maryland rye, as always. Both requests were quickly honored.

As Longarm drank, he studied Jasper Millard with the same frankness with which the bald man was appraising him. Millard practically radiated power, and his eyes glittered with ruthlessness. Longarm had already spotted several bouncers lounging around the room, but he had no doubt that Millard could handle troublemakers every bit as well as his hired help.

Holding his glass of bourbon, Clement turned away from the bar and said excitedly, "I'm going to try my luck at the roulette wheel. Come along, Annie."

"You know, Paul," said Annie, "there might be other things which I wished to do more than watch you gamble."

"But you are my lucky charm!" Clement reached out and grabbed Annie's hand. "Come, *cherie,* the wheel awaits."

Annie gave Longarm a look of resignation and allowed her brother to steer her away from the bar and toward one of the roulette wheels. Clement crowded up to the table and reached into an inner pocket for a wallet. He took several bills from it and dropped them on the table as the croupier prepared to spin the wheel. He was still clasping Annie's hand, and he grinned over at her excitedly as the wheel spun and the ball danced madly around it.

Longarm stayed at the bar and sipped his rye, but he turned so that he could watch the Clements while he did it. With a glance at Millard, he said, "Paul seems to know how to enjoy himself, but I'm not sure he should be waving that billfold around. Never knew who might be watching."

"M'sieu Clement—and his money—are perfectly safe in here," said Millard, "and on the street outside too. That wouldn't be true of most people, mind you. But the denizens

26

of Gallatin Street know that he and his sister are my friends. They know that if anyone were to harm them in any way, I would know who the guilty party was within an hour, and my vengeance would be terrible to behold.''

"You mean they've got friends in high places, so to speak.''

Millard smiled humorlessly. "Most people would consider my associates and me to be friends in *low* places.''

Longarm shrugged and said, "All a matter of perspective, I reckon.''

"You're a Westerner,'' Millard said as he came closer to Longarm. "I can tell.''

"I've spent considerable time west of the Mississippi,'' admitted Longarm, "but I was born and raised in West-by-God Virginia. Started to drift and make my own way after the war.''

"You fought in that unfortunate conflict?''

"Yep, but don't ask me on which side. I tend to disremember.''

Millard chuckled. "As do I, sir, as do I. There are some allegiances a businessman can't afford to maintain, however much he might like to.''

Longarm nodded sagely and said nothing. At the roulette table, Paul Clement threw back his head and grimaced as the ball dropped into a slot and the wheel slowly came to a stop. Longarm heard Clement say, "That's always the way. You play the black, and the red comes up.'' Beside him, Annie just looked bored. She cast occasional glances in Longarm's direction.

With a sly grin, Millard commented, "Mademoiselle Clement seems a bit taken with you, my friend.''

Longarm was about to ask Millard when they had become friends, but he never got around to it.

The sudden screams and the deafening bang of gunshots sort of distracted him.

Chapter 4

Longarm twisted instinctively toward the entrance, where the unexpected disturbance was coming from. He had worn his gun tonight, like most of the other men in the Brass Pelican, and his hand flashed toward the butt of the Colt as he saw the massive doorman Luther stumble into the building, clutching his belly as blood welled between his fingers. The crowd happened to part so that Longarm had a good view of the wounded man, who had obviously been gutshot.

"Look out, Mr. Millard!" shouted Luther. "Royale—"

A man in a derby hat with a bandanna tied over the lower half of his face stepped into the club behind Luther and brought up a pistol, aiming it at the back of the doorman's head. The weapon cracked spitefully, and Luther jerked and pitched forward, dead before he hit the floor, the back of his head a gory mess from the bullet that had just bored into his brain.

"Son of a bitch!" snapped Millard. He practically dived for the area behind the bar and came up with a sawed-off shotgun.

The scattergun would be worse than useless in these close,

crowded quarters, thought Longarm, and he hoped Millard had the sense not to fire it. Too many innocent people would be hurt if he did. The room was filled with chaos now as more of the masked, derby-hatted figures rushed into the club brandishing guns. The crowd of gamblers tried desperately to get out of the line of fire. Some dived under tables while others stampeded wildly, trampling anyone smaller who got in their way.

Longarm glanced toward the roulette table where Annie and Paul Clement had been a moment earlier. He saw no sign of either of them in the mob and hoped they hadn't fallen. If they had, they might be stomped to death. More shots blasted out as Millard's men opened fire on the intruders. Luckily, the bouncers were armed with pocket pistols, but there was still way too much lead flying around to suit Longarm. He saw an expensively gowned woman go spinning off her feet as a stray bullet struck her in the shoulder. As she fell, she screamed thinly and clutched at the sudden bloodstain on her dress.

Men jostled Longarm roughly from both sides. He realized he had to get out of this press of terrified people if he intended to do anything about the situation. Though he knew it would make him a better target for anybody who wanted to take a potshot at him, he slapped his free hand on the bar top and vaulted onto the hardwood. His boots thudded on the mahogany as he ran nimbly along the bar toward the front of the room, bringing him closer to the marauders in derby hats.

The aim of the intruders seemed to be to wreak as much havoc as possible. While some of them were fighting with Millard's bouncers, others were overturning gaming tables and smashing light fixtures. A couple of them grabbed one of the women and literally ripped the clothes off her body, leaving her naked and screaming. Others who wielded clubs and blackjacks waded into the Brass Pelican's patrons, battering several men to the floor. Longarm stopped and snapped a shot at one of the raiders, who was about to bring a hobnailed boot down on the skull of a man who had been knocked off his feet. The stomping would have almost surely been fatal had not Longarm's bullet caught the man in the body and sent him to the floor.

The shot brought return fire, and Longarm crouched as slugs whipped around his head. He triggered twice more and saw one of the gunmen go down. The ebb and flow of the riot sent a knot of people surging between Longarm and the men who were shooting at him, and he used the momentary respite to lunge farther along the bar.

More gunshots from the rear of the club made him throw a glance over his shoulder. He bit back a curse as he saw that more of the masked men were pouring into the place from the back rooms, where they had undoubtedly gained entrance through an alley door. The patrons and employees of the Brass Pelican were caught in a cross fire now.

Millard still stood near the end of the bar. He had traded the sawed-off shotgun for a bungstarter, and he used it to slash at the heads of any of the intruders who came within arm's reach. However, he didn't see the two men who were coming up behind him, guns poised to ambush him.

"Millard!" bellowed Longarm, his voice cutting through the chaos of the attack. "Get down!"

Millard's eyes widened as he saw Longarm twisting back toward him. Longarm threw himself flat on the bar as Millard ducked. That gave Longarm a clear shot at the men who were trying to kill the club owner. He triggered twice, the explosions coming so close together they almost sounded like one blast. The two intruders rocked back as Longarm's bullets thudded into their chests.

That was all Longarm had time to see, because in the next instant hands grabbed him and pulled him off the bar. He felt himself falling and reached out desperately, knowing that if he tumbled all the way to the floor, he would probably never get up again. His fingers snagged the vest of the man who had jerked him off the bar. His fall broken, Longarm lashed his empty Colt across the face of his opponent and felt the man's nose pulp under the blow. Warm blood spurted across the back of Longarm's hand.

He got his feet underneath him and struck again, clubbing at the man's head with the gun. The intruder's derby kept the blow from landing with full force, but it was still powerful enough to make the man's eyes roll up in their sockets as he went limp in Longarm's grasp. Longarm let go of him and let him fall.

He turned, looking for another opponent, and saw a knobby fist coming straight at his face. There was no time to avoid it completely, but he moved his head aside enough so that the blow only grazed him and knocked him back against the bar. He was grateful for the solid hardwood, which kept him from falling. He was able to block the next punch and strike back, reversing the Colt in his hand and using the butt to hammer the face of his attacker. The man stumbled backward, moaning, and was lost in the mob.

The booming of shotguns and the shrilling of whistles assaulted Longarm's ears. He looked toward the entrance and saw blue-uniformed figures bulling their way inside. The New Orleans police had finally arrived. At the sight of the police, the masked men broke off their wave of death and destruction and headed for the back door of the club. No one was left to stop their flight. Millard's bouncers were all down, and none of the Brass Pelican's patrons wanted to interfere. They were concerned only with saving their own skins.

There was nothing Longarm could do either. Too many people surrounded him on all sides. The best he could manage was to holster his gun and wait to see what would happen.

And look for Annie and Paul Clement while he was waiting. Concern for their safety gnawed at him.

The sounds of battle died away. The intruders had made good their escape. But they had left carnage and devastation behind them. Several women still sobbed softly, caught in

31

the grip of fear. Men cursed bitterly and did some sobbing of their own.

Millard shoved several men aside and shouldered his way roughly through the crowd to confront one of the policemen. The badge-toter was as burly as Millard himself, and he had a bulldog face and a thick graying mustache. Millard glowered at him and said loudly, "Damn it, Denton, you and your boys sure as hell took your time about getting here!"

The officer was just as angry and stubborn as Millard. "You can't expect us to come into this hellhole you call Gallatin Street with any less than a full squad!" he blazed back at the club owner. "When the report of trouble came in, I rounded up my men and got here as soon as I could."

Millard waved an arm at the wreckage around him. "Not soon enough to keep Royale's men from busting in here and ruining my place! They killed Luther, damn it, and who knows who else is dead!"

Longarm turned his back on Millard and the policeman called Denton. He pushed his way through the crowd toward the roulette table where he had last seen Annie and her brother. As he came up to the table, he saw that one leg of it had been broken, so that it tilted sharply down to the floor on one corner. Longarm didn't care about that. What mattered to him was that he saw Annie and Clement standing on the other side of the busted table. Both of them were pale and shaken, but other than that, they appeared to be all right.

Annie cried, "Custis!" when she saw him, and Longarm made his way through the crowd to her side. She clutched at his arm, and he said over the hubbub, "Are you hurt?"

She shook her head. "No, Paul and I are fine. How about you?"

"Knocked around a mite, but I'll be fine."

"That is what happened to us too, M'sieu Parker," said Clement as he slid a protective arm around Annie's shoulders. "Annie was very frightened."

"You got any idea who those fellas were?" asked Longarm. "I heard the name Royale a couple of times. I guess it's a name anyway."

Clement nodded grimly. "It is indeed. A *nom de guerre,* to be sure, belonging to one of the cleverest criminals currently operating in New Orleans."

Longarm filed away that bit of information with interest. If Millard was actually connected with one of the smuggling rings, as rumor had it, then this attack tonight had likely been carried out by a rival gang. What Clement had said about the individual known as Royale supported that theory.

Nodding toward the bar, Longarm asked, "Who's the badge-toter jawing with Millard?"

"That's Captain Denton of the New Orleans police," said Clement.

"Appears the two of 'em don't get along very well."

Clement summoned up a laugh. "Captain Denton fancies himself an honest man, which makes him something of a rarity on the New Orleans force. He'd like nothing better than to close down the Brass Pelican for good. However, Jasper has friends who are well connected at City Hall, which makes it impossible for Denton to really do anything to him. I believe the situation frustrates the poor captain to no end."

Longarm told himself to remember what Clement had just said about Captain Denton. If Longarm was in bad enough trouble and needed a helping hand from an honest lawman, he might have to reveal his true identity to someone like Denton . . . and then hope that he would be believed. Supposedly, only the special prosecutor was aware of the password "Pikes Peak" and what it signified.

Beside the bar, Denton turned away from Millard with a curt, angry gesture and began gathering his men, who had spread out through the club with their shotguns. Unfortunately, anyone who might need a greener used on them was long gone. Denton and the other officers began trooping out of the club. Pausing near the door, Denton pointed his shotgun toward Luther's sprawled, bloody corpse and growled, "Bring him along for the undertaker." A couple of the policemen bent and grasped Luther's fancy coat, which was now sodden with blood, and began dragging him out of the club. An ugly red and gray stain was left on the sawdust-littered planks of the floor.

"Hey!" Millard called to Denton. When the captain looked back, Millard pointed to the two men Longarm had killed. "What about these bastards?"

"I'll send a wagon for them," replied Denton wearily.

"The hell you will! I want 'em out of here now."

Denton sighed and motioned for more of his men to retrieve the other two corpses. With grunts and groans of effort, all of the bodies were soon hauled out of the place. Other men had suffered wounds in the melee, but none of them had proven fatal. Some of the women who worked for Millard were already patching up cuts and scrapes and bullet holes with practiced ease that spoke of repeated trouble in the club. The woman whose clothes had been torn off of her was still sobbing, but at least she was no longer naked. Someone had wrapped a frock coat around her, and her escort was leading her to one of the tables that was still upright and undamaged.

Millard jumped up onto the bar, the ease with which he did so rivaling that of Longarm's earlier move. He lifted his hands and shouted for attention. "All right, folks, it's all over! No need to worry anymore! We're going to set things right as quick as we can, so that you can go back to enjoying yourselves! In the meantime, drinks are on the house!"

Some of the club's patrons had been on their way to the door, but they stopped when they heard that offer. Slowly, like the tide running out, nearly everyone in the place began heading toward the bar. Millard hopped down behind it and took off his coat, rolling up his shirt sleeves so that he could help his bartenders pour drinks.

"Well, it shouldn't be long before things are back to normal," Paul Clement said to Longarm. "It's not as if this is the first time Royale's men have caused trouble for Jasper."

"The feud's been going on a long time, eh?" said Long-arm.

"For over a year."

Annie shuddered. "This is the only thing I don't like about coming to the Brass Pelican. There's always the possibility of trouble."

"Ah, but that's part of the appeal of the place," said her brother. "One never knows what is going to happen."

"Some uncertainty I can live without!" said Annie.

Clement took her arm and steered her toward the bar. "Let's go get that free drink Jasper offered," he said. "Who knows how long such generosity will last?"

Longarm trailed along behind them, surveying the damage to the club along the way. Several of the tables were broken, and some of the chairs had been reduced to kindling. The green baize top of one of the poker tables had been ripped to shreds with a knife. The light in the place was dimmer than ever, since several of the fixtures had been shattered. It was damn lucky that a fire hadn't broken out, thought Long-arm. Broken oil lamps were bad about starting blazes.

As for the human toll, none of Millard's bouncers had escaped unscathed. All of them had minor bullet wounds, or lumps on their heads from the clubbing, or both. Half a dozen or more of the customers had been hurt too. The most serious injury appeared to be the bullet wound in the shoulder suffered by the woman Longarm had seen go down early in the attack. She was being tended to by a heavyset man in evening clothes. Longarm nudged Paul Clement, nodded toward the man, and asked, "Who's that?"

"Doctor Deveraux, of course," replied Clement. "He's one of the best-known physicians in New Orleans."

Longarm grunted. Clearly, a respected doctor thought nothing of being caught in a gambling den like the Brass Pelican. Folks here in the Crescent City had their own way of looking at things, that was for sure. What would have been a scandal in a lot of places was just an everyday occurrence here.

The area in front of the bar was still very crowded, but Longarm and the Clements managed to finally make their way up to the hardwood. They found themselves opposite Jasper Millard, who continued to work alongside his bartenders. He stopped short in what he was doing, however, and pointed a blunt finger at Longarm. "You!" he said. "I want to talk to you."

Longarm felt a moment of . . . not apprehension, exactly. Puzzlement was more like it. Millard sounded angry.

Instead of harsh words, though, the club owner extended a hand across the bar to Longarm and suddenly grinned. "You saved my life, Parker!" he said. "I just want you to know I won't forget it."

Longarm returned the handshake, which was just as crushing as the one before. He nodded to Millard and said, "I never did like to see a fella being bushwhacked, and that's sure as hell what those gents had in mind."

"Yeah," said Millard as he released Longarm's hand. He frowned in thought for a moment, then jerked his head toward the door at the end of the bar. "Let's go back to my office. Paul, you and Annie can come along too since you're the ones who brought Parker here tonight."

Clement looked excited at the prospect of visiting Millard's office. He said, "We'll take you up on that invitation, Jasper. Come along, Annie."

Annie seemed less enthused at the idea of joining Millard in the club owner's office, but as usual, she went along with her brother. Longarm had already figured out that Annie might sometimes give in to impulses of her own when she was alone, as when she had invited him to join them tonight, but whenever she was with Paul, he called the shots.

Now that the crush at the bar had lessened somewhat, Millard was able to leave it to his bartenders to handle things. He shrugged back into his coat and led Longarm, Clement, and Annie through the door and into a rear hallway. Several doors opened off the corridor. At the far end was a door leading out to a dark alley. That was the entrance that the second wave of Royale's men had used. From the looks of the splintered jamb, they had kicked their way in. Millard already had a couple of men standing guard there, both of them armed with greeners.

Millard led Longarm, Clement, and Annie through another door, this one opening into a luxuriously appointed office. A large desk was the main item of furniture inside the office, but there were also several chairs upholstered in dark leather. Bookshelves, a liquor cabinet, and another cabinet containing several shotguns lined the walls. A lamp on the desk was burning low, and the shadows were thick in the corners of the room. There were no windows, and Longarm wondered if that was so no one could take a shot at Millard through them. A man like Millard had to lead a worrisome life.

With a sigh, Millard lowered himself into the chair behind the desk and gestured for his guests to take the other chairs. Clement held Annie's chair for her. When everyone was seated, Millard reached into one of the desk drawers and brought out a bottle and some glasses. "This is my best cognac," he said. His eyes lifted to meet Longarm's. "I'd be honored to have you join me, sir. And you and Annie too, of course, Paul."

"Much obliged," said Longarm with a nod. He reached into his vest pocket for a cheroot.

Millard paused in pouring the cognac to gently push a fine wooden box across the desk. "Try one of those, Parker. I get a shipment of them from Havana every month."

Longarm lifted the lid of the box and took out a cigar. He sniffed it appreciatively, broke the band on it, and stuck it in his mouth. As Longarm scratched a lucifer into life, Paul Clement leaned forward and helped himself to one of the cigars too. Millard didn't seem to mind. Longarm puffed on his smoke and got it going, but Clement just tucked his away in a pocket for later. Millard handed glasses of cognac across the desk.

"To timely arrivals," said the club owner as he lifted his drink. Longarm nodded, wondering what Millard meant by that. He found out soon enough, because Millard went on, "I'm talking about you, Parker."

Longarm sipped his cognac and grinned. "You mean the way I was able to stop those two old boys from ventilating you? Hell, that was just good luck."

"And good shooting," grunted Millard. "But I don't really believe in luck, Parker. I believe in Fate. It had to be Fate that brought you here to New Orleans just when I was looking for a man like you."

Longarm frowned. "You mean—"

"I mean, how would you like to go to work for me?"

Chapter 5

Longarm tried not to stare across the desk at Millard. Good luck was still playing into his hands. He had wanted to work in amongst the smugglers, and here and now, on his first night in New Orleans, one of the reputed ringleaders was offering him a job.

Once again, Longarm's brain swiftly considered the possibility that he was being set up somehow. He came to the same conclusion he'd come to earlier when he was pondering Annie's invitation to join her and her brother tonight. There was simply no way that anyone in New Orleans could know who he really was. Fortune had merely been on his side so far on this assignment.

Which was enough to make him a mite nervous, he reflected. Good luck couldn't be depended upon, because it could run out at any time with no warning.

Those thoughts ran through his head in a matter of seconds, but the pause was long enough to prompt Millard to ask, "Well? How about it, Parker?"

Longarm nodded. "I appreciate the offer, Mr. Millard. Like I told you, I'm sort of between jobs."

"Does that mean you accept?"

"I sure do," Longarm told him.

"Without even asking what it is I want you to do?"

Longarm grinned easily. "I figure whatever it is, I'll be able to handle it all right."

Millard gave a short bark of laughter and said, "That's what I figure too."

"Despite the trouble, this evening has worked out well all around, I'd say," Paul Clement put in.

Millard scowled. "I don't know that I'd go that far. This business with Royale . . ." He shook his head, and the hand that wasn't holding the glass of cognac tightened into a fist.

"Tell me about Royale," said Longarm. "I reckon if I'm going to be working for you, I'd best know what's going on."

"I tell my people what they need to know, and that's all," growled Millard. His tone softened a little as he went on. "However, since I'm counting on you to be my right-hand man, Parker, I suppose you *do* have a right to know about Royale. Hell, I won't be giving away any secrets. Practically the whole town knows that we're enemies, Royale and I."

"Who is he?" asked Longarm.

Millard shook his head. "Nobody really knows. Nobody I've ever talked to has even seen him. I've gotten my hands on a couple of men who worked for him, and even *they* don't know who he really is or what he looks like." He scowled in frustration. "And I know how to ask questions that get honest answers too."

I'll just bet you do, old son, thought Longarm, but he kept the comment to himself. Aloud, he said, "Sounds like some kind of mystery man."

"Exactly. But as you saw tonight, it's no mystery what Royale wants. He wants to put me out of business."

"You reckon he owns another gambling club?"

"I don't think so." Millard glanced at the Clements. "The Brass Pelican isn't my only business. I have . . . other enterprises." It was clear that he didn't want to speak too openly

40

about those enterprises in front of Annie and her brother.

Clement took the hint. He drained the last of his cognac and reached for Annie's hand as he stood up. "If it's all right with you, Jasper," he said smoothly, "Annie and I will go back out and see if the roulette wheel is functioning again. You know me—all this talk of business bores me."

Millard waved a hand toward the door. "Sure, go ahead. Just one thing, Paul . . ."

Clement and Annie paused at the doorway. "Yes?"

"Thanks for bringing Parker with you tonight."

"It was our pleasure," said Clement with a grin.

Annie looked at Longarm and said, "I'll see you later, I suppose, Custis."

"I reckon you can count on that," Longarm told her sincerely.

Annie and Clement left the office. When they were gone, Longarm leaned back in his chair and puffed on the cigar while Millard refilled their glasses. "Martell," the club owner said, indicating the label on the cognac bottle. "The finest in the world. I bring it in from France."

"The same way you bring in cigars from Cuba?" guessed Longarm.

Millard's quick grin told Longarm he was right. "I don't pay customs duty on either one of them, if that's what you mean. They come in through the Delta."

"So one of those other business enterprises you mentioned is smuggling."

"That bother you?" asked Millard bluntly.

Longarm took another puff on the cigar and shook his head. "Nope. Not even a little bit."

"When I saw how handy with that gun you are, I knew you were the sort of man who wouldn't let anything stand in his way. That's good." Millard sipped his cognac and looked intently at Longarm over the glass, then added, "As long as you're not *too* ambitious."

"When I take a man's money, I back him all the way," Longarm said with conviction.

"Good." Millard leaned back in his own chair. "Royale runs a smuggling ring, just like I do. He'd like to see me dead, and I'm convinced that raid tonight was just a cover for an attempt to kill me. I was supposed to die in the confusion."

Longarm nodded slowly. "I can see that. Those two gunmen came straight for you while the rest of 'em were raising hell."

"That's right. And if the attempt failed—which, thanks to you, it did—at least Royale hurt me a little by damaging my club."

Longarm had no doubt that Millard was right, but he said, "Do you know for sure that Royale was behind what happened tonight?"

Millard snorted in disgust. "Of course Royale was behind it. Nobody else moves a fraction as many goods through the Delta as Royale and I do. Our organizations control the smuggling now. If Royale could get rid of me, he'd have the whole thing right in his hands." The club owner shrugged his burly shoulders. "Besides, Royale's men always wear those derbies and have masks over their faces. It's like a badge."

"Speaking of badges, how does Captain Denton feel about Royale?"

With a harsh laugh, Millard replied, "Denton hates Royale as much as he hates me. He'd like to see Royale behind bars—or dead, same as me. That stupid bastard actually thinks he can clean up New Orleans if he works at it hard enough." Millard laughed again. "But it'll never happen. This town doesn't *want* to be cleaned up. Nobody really gives a damn about the law."

That was where he was wrong, thought Longarm. Somebody cared about the law—even if he was from out of town.

"So Denton can't bother you because of your connections, and he can't get to Royale either, I'd wager. Any trouble from any of the other local lawmen, or any federal boys?" The way the conversation had been going, Longarm didn't

42

think it was too much of a risk to pose the question. After all, if he was going to work for Millard, he had a right to know what he was getting into.

Millard shook his bald head. "Nothing to speak of. Nothing we can't handle."

"Sounds good," said Longarm with a nod, concealing his disappointment. But it would have been too much to hope for if Millard had upped and confessed to killing Douglas Ramsey just like that. Still, there had been a chance that he would, since he was feeling expansive and grateful to Longarm for saving his life.

But maybe Millard *wasn't* responsible for Ramsey's murder. Maybe Royale or some of his men had been the ones who had put the knife in Ramsey's back and then dumped him in the bayou. Longarm would just have to keep poking around until he knew for sure, and the unexpected foothold he had gained in Millard's organization was the perfect place for him to start.

Millard tossed back the rest of his drink and set the empty glass on the desk with a thump. "I'm going down in the Delta tomorrow," he said. "I want you to come with me, Parker. I'll show you the ropes, and it won't take long for you to catch on to the way we do things down here."

Longarm finished his cognac. "I'll be looking forward to it," he said honestly. "You expecting any more trouble from Royale?"

Millard grinned coldly across the desk at him. "I don't know. But if we run into any, you'll be there to handle it, won't you?"

Most of the damage in the main room of the gambling club had been put right with surprising speed. The broken tables had been propped up, a cloth had been spread over the poker table with the slashed top, and the games were under way again when Longarm and Millard left the office a few minutes later.

Paul Clement had left the roulette wheel for the blackjack

table. Annie was still at his side, one of her hands held firmly in both of his except when he had to let go to push chips up to the betting line. Unobtrusively, Longarm watched him play several hands. Clement was a plunger, Longarm decided, unable to stay even when the odds were on his side. On nearly every hand, he leaned forward and said in a breathless voice, "Hit me," succumbing to the siren call of the next card, whatever it might be. Not surprisingly, he lost more than he won, though he hit blackjack a couple of times and exclaimed happily.

Annie glanced over her shoulder and saw Longarm watching them. She slipped her hand out of her brother's grip, and Clement looked over at her sharply, almost angrily. Longarm saw her say something in his ear, and after a second, he nodded grudgingly. Annie walked toward Longarm with a smile.

"I told Paul that all the excitement earlier has given me a headache," she said as she came up to him. "I thought perhaps you would accompany me back to our mansion."

"I'd be happy to," Longarm told her, "but isn't that something your brother really ought to do?"

Annie made a face. "Paul would never forgive me if I dragged him away from his games of chance so early in the evening. He probably won't stop playing until the sun comes up. You can take me home, then return here or go back to the St. Charles, whatever you wish. The driver will come back here to get Paul later."

Longarm nodded. "All right. Let's go."

Annie stopped long enough to get her lacy shawl from the cloak room. She wrapped it around her shoulders as they stepped outside. The evening's festivities on Gallatin Street were still in full swing. The warm night air was full of tinny music and shrill laughter.

The black carriage was waiting nearby at the curb. Longarm helped Annie in, then said to the wizened driver, "The lady wants to go home. I'll be going with her, then back to the St. Charles."

44

He swung up into the carriage, and was about to sit on the front seat when Annie said, "Sit beside me, Custis."

"Always glad to oblige a lady," he said with a grin as he settled down on the rear seat next to her.

"I'm very glad to hear that." Her voice had an undertone that was almost a purr.

Almost instantly, Longarm felt himself growing aroused. Annie was sitting close enough to him that he could feel the warmth of her body, and her perfume, subtle yet insistent, filled his senses. She reached over and caught hold of his hand, twining her fingers with his.

"I am so glad I met you today, Custis, and that you were with us tonight at the club. When those horrible men came bursting in, I was frightened, and yet . . . I knew I would be all right. I knew you wouldn't allow any harm to come to me."

She was giving him more credit than he was due. In the confusion of the raid, with all those bullets flying around, almost anything could have happened to her, and likely there wouldn't have been a damned thing he could have done to stop it.

But she *had* come through the violence all right, and if she wanted to think that he was partially responsible for that, he supposed it wouldn't hurt anything. "I'm glad I was there too," he told her. "It means a lot to me, the way you and your brother have sort of taken me under your wing."

She laughed, but didn't sound particularly amused. "You won't need our help anymore, now that you're working for Jasper Millard. He's one of the most powerful men in New Orleans."

"Him and that fella Royale, huh?"

A tiny shudder ran through Annie's body. "Don't even talk about Royale. He . . . he frightens me."

"But you don't have any real connection with Millard except patronizing his club, do you?" asked Longarm.

"No, of course not, but you saw what happened tonight.

45

As long as Jasper and Royale are at each other's throat, no one in New Orleans is really safe.''

She had a point, thought Longarm. He had seen other towns where two or more factions of owlhoots had been feuding, and what usually happened was that more innocent folks were killed in the fighting than members of the opposing outlaw gangs. It was the same here in New Orleans. Everyone was at risk while the war between Millard and Royale continued.

He would just have to see what he could do about that, Longarm decided. Though his real job was to find out who killed Douglas Ramsey, maybe at the same time he could bust up the smuggling rings and put an end to the rivalry between Millard and Royale. Of course, somebody else would probably just come along and take their places later, but that was out of Longarm's hands. He couldn't be responsible for ridding the world of *all* its crooks and killers.

After a few minutes, the carriage reached Chartres Street and rolled through an open gate of black wrought iron onto a circular drive paved with flagstones. It led up to the entrance of a large, three-story brick house. Wooden pillars bordered a veranda that ran the length of the house. The pillars supported a balcony with moss dripping from its railing. The mansion was old but well kept, Longarm saw with a glance as the carriage came to a stop.

He opened the door and stepped down, then turned back to assist Annie. As she took his hand, she whispered, ''Come in with me.''

Longarm wasn't particularly surprised. All during the carriage ride, if not before that, he had been able to tell that Annie was attracted to him. The feeling was mutual. But he murmured softly, ''I told the driver to take me back to the hotel.''

''Ask him to return to the Brass Pelican and wait for Paul,'' she said. ''Tell him that you will walk back to the St. Charles.''

The lie seemed pretty apparent to Longarm, but at least it

would allow Annie to keep up appearances. He moved to the front of the carriage and looked up at the driver. "You can head on back to the club and wait for Mr. Clement, old son," he told the man. "It's a nice night, so I think I'll walk over to my hotel from here."

"As you wish, suh," said the driver as he took up his reins once more. "Good evenin' to yuh."

With a gentle flick of the reins, the driver got the team moving again, and the carriage rolled on around the drive and back through the gate onto Chartres Street. Longarm turned around and looked at Annie, who was standing at the door underneath the small lamp that had been left burning there. In its soft yellow glow, she looked incredibly lovely. She lifted a hand, held it out toward Longarm.

He went to her, clasping her hand, and she led him into the house.

Inside, the mansion matched its opulent exterior. Hand in hand, Longarm and Annie moved through a foyer with gilt-edged mirrors on both walls that opened into a large, airy room with a high ceiling. When Longarm glanced up, he saw that the chamber extended all the way to a large domed skylight in the mansion's roof. A curving staircase with an alabaster rail led up to a balcony that ran completely around the central room. He could see a third-floor balcony as well. Annie tugged him toward the stairs, a little impatient now.

"I thought I was supposed to walk back to the St. Charles," he said dryly.

"Don't toy with me, Custis," she said. "We both know why I asked you to come in. My bedroom is on the third floor."

"Usually in cases like this, it's the lady who says something about how things are moving sort of fast."

She laughed, a liquid, sensual sound. "As I told you, don't toy with me. I want you, Custis Parker, and I intend to have you."

As they reached the bottom of the staircase and Annie took a step up, Longarm said, "Your brother . . ."

47

She whirled back toward him, her features taut and unreadable. "Don't talk about Paul," she said. "Don't even mention him. Not tonight."

Longarm frowned. He wasn't sure what had come over Annie. Earlier in the evening, she had seemed devoted to her brother, even though she was a little bored by his gambling. Now she acted almost as if she hated him.

But that was none of his business, Longarm told himself. He had been lucky enough to meet this beautiful woman, and now she wanted him in her bed and was completely unabashed about her desires. His chance acquaintance with Annie and Paul Clement had already paid a considerable dividend in the job he had landed with Jasper Millard. Now he seemed to be on the verge of collecting another dividend.

The fact that she was standing on the first step while he was still on the floor brought their faces close to the same level. Suddenly, Annie leaned forward, and her lips found his in an urgent kiss. Longarm slipped his arms around her waist and pulled her to him.

His tongue darted between her lips as she opened herself to him, and he explored the hot, wet cavern of her mouth for several moments. Her tongue replied in kind, circling his, fencing with it. Her breasts prodded softly against his chest, and her arms tightened around his neck as she hugged him.

They stood that way for a long moment, straining against each other. Then Annie broke the kiss. "Come!" she said urgently. She reached down to catch hold of his hand. "Come with me."

Longarm went.

A few minutes later, he found himself in an elegantly furnished bedchamber on the third floor of the mansion. There were lace curtains on the windows and a thick rug on the floor. The room was dominated by the large, four-poster, canopied bed that was its main piece of furniture, but there was also a long dressing table with a mirror above it and a tall wardrobe with gold handles on its doors. Annie tugged him eagerly toward the bed.

Longarm stopped her and turned her around so that her back was toward him. His fingers went to the buttons of the gown and began unfastening them. With all the buttons behind her like this, he knew she hadn't done up this gown herself; she must have had help, and that made him wonder about servants. He leaned closer to her and whispered into her ear, "Any hired help in the house?"

She closed her eyes and leaned back against him as she shook her head. "They've all gone home for the night. None of them stay here. We have the house to ourselves."

Longarm went back to what he was doing, which was unfastening the final button in the row that ran down her spine. He spread the dress open, revealing the smooth, honey-colored expanse of her back all the way down to the sensual twin dimples just above the cleft of her buttocks. He gathered up the thick masses of her hair and lifted them to expose the nape of her neck, and that was where he planted his lips in a long, lingering kiss that slowly slid down her back. Annie shivered and made a noise deep in her throat. He heard her whisper his name.

When he reached the small of her back, he stopped and let his tongue play over the smooth skin and downy hairs he found there. After a moment in which her breathing became noticeably heavier, Annie moved a step away from him and turned. Longarm stayed where he was, kneeling on the soft rug beside the bed. He looked up at her as she pulled the dress over her shoulders and then slowly lowered it in front of her. Her firm, apple-shaped breasts came into view. They rode high and proud on her chest, and the large brown nipples were pebbled and erect.

She pushed the gown on past her hips, taking her petticoats with it. As the frilly undergarments fell around her ankles, she stood nude before him. Longarm gloried in her loveliness, his heart beating heavily in his chest. He stood slowly and stepped over to her. She held out her arms to receive him. He kissed her again, savoring the erotic sensation of cradling her naked form against him while he was still fully dressed.

That situation didn't last long. Her fingers fairly flew over his body as she began taking his clothes off, unbuttoning here, tugging there, her movements becoming more urgent as she stripped away the layers of fabric separating his skin from hers. Finally, her hand closed around the huge pole of flesh that jutted out from his groin, and she sighed as her eyes widened in wonder.

Her back was to the bed, and as Longarm rested his hands on her bare shoulders and pressed down gently, she went eagerly, reclining and pulling him down with her. Her thighs parted and his hand found her core, which was already drenched in her juices. She clutched his shaft with both hands, making milking motions along it as his fingers delved into the wet folds of feminine flesh. The ball of his hand was resting on her mound, and he pressed down gently but insistently. She took one hand away from his erection and caught hold of his hair as he lowered his head to one of her hard, demanding nipples and sucked it into his mouth. His shaft was like a rod of iron, throbbing almost painfully as she caressed it and used her thumb to spread the moisture that pearled from its tip all around the flaring head.

"Now, Custis!" she gasped. "Oh, God, now!"

He had already moved between her widespread thighs, balancing there on his knees. His manhood was only inches away from her fiery center. He drove forward with a thrust of his hips and found the gates of her womanhood open wide for him. She gasped again as he entered her, filling her deeply and completely. She wrapped her arms and legs around him and held on to him with surprising strength. The muscles of her femininity clenched on him as well, their grip so hot and tight that he almost lost control right away.

With a groan of effort, he exerted his iron will and forced down the reaction that was building within him. Neither of them were ready for this to be over yet. His hips began to move as he withdrew almost all the way, then plunged into her again.

"Harder!" she panted. "Harder!"

Longarm drove in and out, filling her to the brim, then pulling back. Both of them were breathing fast now, and Longarm could hear the thunder of his pulse inside his head. Annie plastered her mouth to his and her tongue shot into his mouth, plundering him as he was plundering her down below. The rest of the world had retreated, leaving only the two of them, and the only sounds to be heard on the entire planet were the rasp of their breath, the liquid movement of heated flesh within flesh, and the faint slapping of belly against belly.

Then Annie tore her mouth away from his and began to make a small, keening sound as her head thrashed from side to side on the bed. Longarm knew she had reached her culmination, so he held back no longer. He plunged deeply within her again, as deep as he could go, and held his shaft there as great, shuddery spasms shook him. His seed exploded from him in spurt after spurt, draining him and filling her in the eternal siphon of passion. Finally, with another shudder and jerk, the last of it welled from him. Sated, he slipped from her and rolled to the side, because he knew that if he didn't get off her, his weight would crush her as his muscles turned to jelly and he could no longer support himself on his elbows and knees.

Annie snuggled against his side, resting her head on his chest as he looped an arm around her and held her to him. Breathlessly, she said, "I am . . . so glad you . . . came to New Orleans, Custis."

He brushed his lips against her hair and murmured, "So am I."

In truth, his first day here had gone stunningly well. He had made progress on the job that had brought him to the Crescent City, and he had bedded a lovely, passionate woman whom he hadn't even known when this morning dawned.

Too much good luck?

Longarm wondered how that trip down to the Delta country with Jasper Millard was going to go the next day.

Chapter 6

Longarm said, "Damn!" and swatted at the mosquito busily feasting on his neck. Beside him, Jasper Millard laughed.

"You stay down here in this country for very long, Parker," said Millard, "and you'll get to where you don't even notice those little bastards."

"That one wasn't so little," Longarm said as he studied the squashed insect on the palm of his hand. Its death had left a smear of blood on his skin. His *own* blood, thought Longarm, which the varmint had just sucked out of him. "These things get much bigger, they're liable to start carrying off dogs."

Millard chuckled again. He and Longarm were riding side by side along a road that followed the twisting course of a bayou. It was midmorning and already quite hot, even though the cypress trees that bordered the road cast quite a bit of shade. Long strands of Spanish moss dangling from the branches brushed against Longarm's face from time to time. A warm breeze that was as lazy as the almost imperceptible current of the bayou brought a mixture of pungent smells to Longarm. The most prominent was that of the rich brown earth, but he also smelled the sweetness of honeysuckle and bougainvillea as well as the sharper tang of rotting fish. All in all, it was a blend that took some getting used to.

He had left his coat and vest behind today, though he still wore the string tie around his neck. His white shirt was already soaked with sweat. He had rolled the sleeves up for a while, but exposing his brawny forearms just gave the mosquitos more places to bite him. The sleeves were rolled down now. He wore brown whipcord pants and his usual black stovepipe boots. Millard had complimented him on the high-topped boots. "They're good for tromping around the bayou country," Millard had said. "Helps keep the rattlers and the cottonmouths and the copperheads and the coral snakes from biting you."

What kind of place was it, Longarm wondered, that had so many venomous snakes? Weren't one or two kinds enough?

The area was teeming with wildlife. So far he had seen deer and squirrels and skunks and opossums. A couple of times he had spotted what he first thought were logs floating in the water, and then he had seen the tiny black eyes protruding from the surface of the bayou. Those were alligators out there, he realized, gators just like the one that had chomped half of Douglas Ramsey's body. Maybe one of them was the *same* gator, for all he knew. A chill went through him at the thought, but he managed not to shudder.

From time to time, Longarm and Millard passed shacks with palmetto-thatched roofs. The shacks were built of unpainted, weather-bleached boards and were set atop stilts, and many of them leaned a little—whether from shoddy construction or the hurricane winds that sometimes blew from the Gulf, Longarm didn't know. Beside the shacks were small patches of garden. Cows and pigs and chickens were confined in ramshackle pens. Some of the shacks backed up to the bayou or even extended over the water on their stilts, and pirogues were tied up at these. The lightweight canoes drew very little water, Longarm knew. He had heard it said that they could float on a heavy dew.

Sometimes narrow, pinched, sunburned faces peered out at the two riders from the windows or porches of the shacks. Millard ignored the Cajuns as he rode past. Longarm felt a pang of sympathy for them, then wondered if the emotion was misplaced. These people who lived in the bayou country were a breed apart in some ways; hard though it might be, this life was the only one they knew, and Longarm suspected that most of them would never be happy anywhere else.

Another bayou joined the one they were following, and the water grew wider to their left. Millard waved at a field of flowers to the right and said, "Looks solid, doesn't it?"

"I reckon it does," said Longarm.

"You wouldn't want to ride across there. You wouldn't make it five feet before your horse was bogged down in mud up to its belly. In fact, almost anywhere you go off this road it would be like that."

Longarm looked around. The landscape appeared to be tallgrass prairie for the most part, sprinkled with fields full of flowers. Even without Millard's warning, though, he would have known from past visits to this area that appearances were deceiving. Any man who strayed off known paths ran the risk of winding up in quicksand or water over his head with little or no warning.

The cypress trees thinned out and gradually vanished, and Longarm and Millard entered a region of long, shallow ridges covered with rows of stunted oaks. "Shinneries," grunted Millard, pointing at the ridges with a thumb. "That's where we'll find the men we're looking for."

A few minutes later, he turned his horse and rode onto one of the ridges that crossed the path. Longarm followed. The shinnery oaks provided a little shade from the sun, which was climbing higher and higher in the sky and growing warmer as it climbed. The cypresses, with their spreading limbs and shawls of Spanish moss, had given better shade, but Longarm was grateful for anything that blocked the blasting rays of the sun.

Ahead of them, the ridge curved gradually to the right, and it appeared to run for several miles. Longarm couldn't see the end of it. It was perhaps a quarter of a mile wide, with salt-grass marshes flanking it on both sides. They had ridden about a mile, Longarm judged, when they came within sight of a cluster of shacks.

There were rivulets of open water among the marshes, and Longarm knew that the men who paddled the pirogues pulled up next to the shacks could navigate the twisting waterways through those marshes and swamps with as much ease and confidence as he could ride from Denver to Cheyenne. At the moment, several men were gathered on the porch of one of the shacks. As Longarm and Millard rode up, the men lifted hands in greeting and one of them stood up to walk slowly out to meet them.

"Howdy, Mr. Millard. We is here like you say, us."

"You have something for me?" asked Millard, not dismounting.

"Always gots something, no? Take it to N'awleans, you, an' sell her for plenty-plenty money, yes?"

"Depends on what you've got."

The man, who was tall and skinny with a thatch of dark hair that fell over his forehead, waved a hand at the pirogues, which were loaded with oilcloth-covered bundles. "We gots fine silk, us, an' a case or three o' wine, an' some o' them fancy see-gars from the Cubanos, you bet. You make us a good price, an' we load her on your wagons when they come, yes."

At the mention of the Cuban cigars, Millard shot a glance at Longarm, as if reminding him of the one he had smoked the night before in the Brass Pelican. Then he looked back at the spokesman for the Cajun smugglers and shook his head solemnly. "There's not enough demand for those goods, boys," he said. "You're going to have to give me a good price on the lot if you want me to take it."

"Our hearts, they are breakin'!" exclaimed the smuggler. "We are poor men, us, jus' tryin' to make a little-little money for our families, no? These words, they hurt us."

Millard shrugged his brawny shoulders, took off his planter's hat, and used a handkerchief he pulled from his pocket to mop sweat from his bald head. "It's up to you, Antoine," he said.

Longarm had seen haggling like this many times before, in border towns from California to Texas. In its own way, this Delta country was like a border town, because there was no place else exactly like it. Arguing over a price was to be expected, and Longarm wasn't surprised when a moment later, the spokesman for the smugglers echoed Millard's shrug and said, "A hard man, you, Mr. Millard, but we takes your money—"

His concession was interrupted by the sudden bark of a gunshot. The Cajun's eyes widened in shock and pain as he stumbled back a couple of steps. A crimson flower of blood bloomed on the breast of his grayish-white shirt.

More shots rang out as the other men exploded from the porch of the shack. Rifles and shotguns had appeared in their grimy hands as if by magic. As the wounded man slumped to the ground, his companions looked around for the source of the attack.

Longarm had twisted in the saddle and drawn his Colt, and beside him, Millard had pulled a gun too. Longarm thought the shot had come from behind them, so he wheeled his horse around.

Figures wearing derby hats and bandannas over their faces were bursting from the tall salt grass onto the shinnery upstream from the cabins, their guns blazing. Two more of the Cajun smugglers went down. Millard roared, "Royale!" and started firing at the masked men. Longarm triggered a couple of shots, and had the satisfaction of seeing one of the men tumble backwards into the marsh with a muddy splash.

"Let's get out of here!" he shouted to Millard, yanking on his horse's reins. "There are too many of them!"

Around two dozen men were attacking the cluster of smugglers' shacks, Longarm estimated, though making an accurate count wasn't the most important thing on his mind in the heat of battle. They must have slipped through the marshes in pirogues until they were in position to strike. Longarm didn't want to abandon the smugglers, but it was vital that he keep Millard alive for the time being, until he found out who had really killed Douglas Ramsey.

Millard didn't seem interested in flight. He was returning the fire of Royale's men as fast as he could. Already a slug had chewed a hole in the crown of his hat, coming within inches of splattering his brains on the ground. Longarm snapped off another shot, then reached over and grabbed hold of Millard's arm.

"Come on, damn it!"

This time, Millard went with Longarm. The two of them galloped past the cabins, heading farther east along the shinnery. That left the Cajun smugglers behind to defend their homes as best they could, and Longarm grimaced as he thought about how outnumbered and outgunned they were. Still, there was nothing he could do about it—

And he and Millard weren't out of trouble yet themselves, he saw a moment later as a group of riders emerged from a stand of the stunted oaks up ahead and rode toward them, firing as they came.

"Son of a bitch!" exclaimed Millard. "There's more of the bastards!"

There was indeed, thought Longarm grimly. Now he and Millard were caught between two forces, and the only way left open to them lay through the treacherous salt marshes.

They had no choice in the matter. If they stayed on the shinnery, they would be dead in a matter of moments, shot to ribbons by Royale's murderous gang.

"Come on!" shouted Longarm as he turned his horse and sent it leaping off the path into the salt grass.

Luck guided him. The ground beneath his horse's hooves was fairly firm at this point. The head-high grass closed around him, cutting him off from the view of the shinnery. Royale's men were able to track his progress through the marsh by the waving of the grass, however, and slugs slashed through the stalks around him. Longarm glanced over his shoulder and saw that Millard was right behind him. Longarm was glad Millard hadn't stayed to fight, because then he would have had to go back and try to pull Millard out of the fire.

Now all they had to do was survive the hail of rifle bullets that was scything through the salt grass around them.

"Be careful, Parker!" Millard shouted suddenly. "You're about to run up on some water—"

He didn't get to finish his warning. Longarm's mount burst from the grass into a narrow open space filled with shallow black water. It splashed up around the horse's hooves, splattering mud on Longarm's boots and trousers. The horse slid to one side, in danger of losing its footing, and Longarm hauled desperately on the reins, as if he could hold the animal up with sheer brute strength. He realized quickly that it was hopeless, and kicked his feet free from the stirrups as the horse fell.

Longarm landed half in the water, half on firmer ground. He managed to keep his pistol aloft so that it didn't get wet or fouled with mud. A few yards away, the horse scrambled to its feet and lunged out of the water, but it took only a few steps before it began to flounder again. Thick black mud sucked at its legs, and as Longarm watched in horror, the animal began to sink. That was not just mud, Longarm realized.

It was quicksand.

There was nothing he could do for the horse. He had no rope, no way to pull it free. Its shrill screams wrenched at him as it was quickly swallowed up by the clinging liquid mud. As the horse's cries died away in a hideous gurgle, Longarm heard men's voices shouting somewhere not far away. "Over here!" one of them yelled. "Quicksand's got the bastard's horse, sure as hell!"

"Maybe got *him* too!" called another man.

Those were Royale's hired killers, thought Longarm as he crouched on the edge of the narrow stream. He looked around for Millard, and bit back a curse. There was no sign of the man. Millard had been right behind him when he hit the water, but he had vanished after that. Longarm thought that he must have chosen another path through the marsh and was still trying to get away from Royale's men. Hoofbeats didn't make much noise on this soft ground, so Longarm couldn't tell if Millard was still on horseback or not.

Millard had abandoned him, he thought with a sardonic grunt. Well, that came as no real surprise. Longarm had known the man less than twenty-four hours, and it wasn't reasonable to expect Millard to risk his own life to stay behind and help a new employee. All Longarm could do now was try to get himself out of this mess and hope that Millard made it back to New Orleans safely.

The voices of the hunters were getting closer now. Longarm had no idea how well Royale's men knew these marshes, but if they knew their way around at all, they were better off than he was. He crouched in the tall grass and lifted his Colt, his hand tightening on the butt of the gun. Outnumbered as he was, he couldn't hope to shoot it out with them and come out alive, but they didn't seem to be interested in taking any prisoners.

"Be careful," said one of the killers, surprisingly close. "I don't know who that fella with Millard was."

"Don't matter," came the harsh reply. "We'll jus' kill him anyway, no matter who he be."

Longarm's lips drew back from his teeth in a grimace. *You can try, old son*, he thought. *You can try*.

Then he had to swallow a startled cry as a hand reached out from the salt grass and grabbed hold of his left arm.

He twisted toward the unknown attacker and jerked his gun around, finger tightening on the trigger. Just in time, his brain registered what his eyes were seeing, and his finger froze, stopping him from putting a bullet through the brain of the young woman who crouched beside him in the mud.

Chapter 7

She put a finger to her lips, motioning to him for silence.

Longarm's eyes widened in surprise. He had never seen this young woman before. If he had, he would have remembered her. He was certain of that.

She was an olive-skinned beauty with thick dark hair tumbling to her shoulders. The thin cotton dress she wore clung wetly to her body, making the nipples on her pear-shaped breasts plainly visible. Once, the dress had been an elegant gown, Longarm saw, but now it was old and ripped in places, and the bottom had been torn off so that it came down only midway on her thighs, leaving the rest of her tanned, muscular legs bare. Her feet were shod in flimsy slippers that were caked with mud, and mud was splattered on her calves too, as well as on her dress. There was even a smear of it on her face. Despite the ragged dress and the grime, she was still lovely.

She tugged on Longarm's sleeve and motioned with her other hand for him to follow her.

Longarm glanced around. The gunmen were still prowling around close by, and within a matter of minutes, they were bound to stumble over him if he didn't move. Even though he had no idea who this young woman was, he was willing to bet that she knew her way around the marsh better than he did. He nodded, letting her know that he was willing to follow her.

He hoped she wasn't planning to lead him into a trap.

Longarm figured he looked like a damned fool as he walked in a crouch after her, but better to look foolish than to stick his head up and get it shot off, he decided. Besides, they traveled that way only for a few yards, Longarm following closely behind the young woman as she carefully parted the salt grass, and then they reached the bank of another stream. A pirogue was there, pulled up on firmer ground. The young woman gestured for Longarm to get in.

He did so, hoping there were no coral snakes or cottonmouths lurking under the surface of the water as he waded into it and stepped up into the pirogue. The young woman pushed the craft off the bank and hopped in lithely. Obviously she had had plenty of practice getting in and out of pirogues.

She picked up a paddle lying in the bottom and dipped it into the water. Longarm checked for another paddle so that he could help, and saw that there wasn't one. Clearly she intended to do all the paddling herself. She gestured for him to keep his head down, then settled into a steady rhythm with the paddle. It bit quietly into the water and pushed them along, first on one side of the pirogue, then the other. The splashes were so faint that Longarm doubted if they could be heard more than a few feet away.

He could still hear Royale's men shouting among themselves as they searched for him and Millard, though, and the growing frustration was plain to hear in their voices. There had been no more shots, which gave Longarm reason to hope that Millard had gotten away. After having such a perfect setup for his investigation fall into his lap, he hated the idea of having to start over if Millard wound up dead at the hands of Royale's men.

More streams intersected the one on which they were traveling, and Longarm quickly grew confused by the twists and turns of the route that the young woman was following. He knew that the shouts of Royale's men were dying away in the distance behind them, however, and for the moment, that was all he cared about. His lovely young rescuer and guide, self-appointed though she might be, was doing an excellent job of getting him out of a whole mess of trouble. Longarm slipped his Colt back in its holster, figuring that he no longer needed it, at least for the time being.

Within half an hour, they were out of the marshes and back in the bayou country, with huge cypresses spreading their limbs over the twisting, slow-moving waterways. Now that she didn't have to worry so much about noise, the young woman paddled with stronger strokes, and the pirogue slid easily over the water.

"I'm mighty obliged for what you did back there," Longarm said, breaking the silence between them. "Reckon you saved my bacon, ma'am."

She turned her head and flashed a dazzling smile at him. "This bay-konn of yours, him is good with the hush puppies, no?" Her Cajun accent was thick, but the words still sounded soft and musical coming from her.

Longarm chuckled. "I suppose you may be right. I'm Custis Parker."

"Cussstisss," she repeated, drawing out the name. "Name is Claudette, mine."

"Well, Claudette, you came along just in time. Those fellas who were looking for me would've found me pretty soon, and when they did they'd have done their best to put some bullets in my hide."

She nodded as she paddled, and without looking back at him, she said, "Knew they wanted to kill you, I did. Heard 'em yellin' 'bout it. Figure any man in so much trouble, gotta help him."

"You know who those other gents were?"

She shrugged her shoulders without breaking the rhythm

of her paddling. "Smuggler men." The distaste in her voice was evident.

"You don't like the smugglers? Lots of folks in this part of the country are mixed up in it, I hear."

Claudette shook her head. "Other people, not me. I catch the crawfish, trap the otter and the nutria for their furs, get by jus' fine."

"What about your family?" asked Longarm.

Again, she shook her head. "Gran'pere the last one left, an' the sickness take him last winter, it did. Now jus' me, but I don't mind."

"Where do you live?"

She brought the paddle back into the pirogue and used her right hand to point. "My home, there."

Longarm leaned over to look past her, and saw that she was pointing at a shack built on the edge of the bayou, part of it extending over the water on its stilts like some of the others he had seen today. This one was surrounded by thick brush and cypress trees, however, so that it seemed even more cut off from the rest of the world as it perched on the edge of the slow-moving water. Claudette turned and smiled at Longarm again, then resumed paddling toward the ramshackle cabin.

There was a crude ladder built on the side of the shack that hung over the water, and Claudette sent the pirogue skimming straight toward it. As they came alongside, she caught hold of the ladder, which led up to a door mounted on sagging leather hinges. She stood up, steadying herself with the ladder, and tied the pirogue to it with a stout cord. Then she climbed up to the door and opened it, and Longarm couldn't help but admire the play of the muscles in her legs and rear end under the thin dress. She looked back over her shoulder and beckoned for Longarm to follow her.

He reached up and grabbed the ladder, waiting until Claudette had disappeared into the cabin before he started up. When he stepped through the open door into the shack, it took a moment for his eyes to adjust to the gloom. Here under the cypress trees, the world was cloaked in perpetual green shadows, but the light was even dimmer inside the cabin. He saw Claudette moving on the other side of the single room, and after a few seconds he could tell that she was starting a fire in an old wood-burning stove.

"Heat you up some gumbo, I will," she said. "He's gonna fill up your belly. Mighty tasty, I guarantee."

Now that she mentioned it, he was getting hungry, Longarm realized. It had been a long time since breakfast in the hotel dining room this morning. He figured it was well past midafternoon, and when he pulled out his watch and flipped the cover open, he saw that he was right.

"Pretty-pretty watch," said Claudette when she saw what he was doing. "Gran'pere, he have him a watch like that. When he die, bury it with him, I did."

"Looks like you could have used it," commented Longarm as he put his own watch away.

Claudette waved a hand to indicate their surroundings and said, "Time, she don't matter here in the bayou country."

Longarm knew what she meant. In this region of heat and water and lush vegetation, this ever-shifting borderland between the sea and the shore, one day was much like the next. There were few changes, few reasons for anyone to know exactly what time it was.

He looked around the inside of the cabin. Besides the stove, it was furnished with a rough-hewn table, several rickety-looking chairs, and a narrow bed with a straw mattress. Through a window in the front wall, he saw a hammock strung between two posts that held up a rotting porch roof.

Claudette noticed him looking around, and she dropped her gaze to the unpainted planks of the floor as she said, "This a mighty sorry place to live, you're thinkin', Custis. And you're right."

Quickly, he shook his head. In truth, he didn't understand how a bright, vital young woman like Claudette could be happy in such squalid surroundings, but he didn't want to hurt her feelings by saying that. After all, she had saved his life, more than likely, and she was about to feed him a bowl of gumbo.

"Everybody's got a right to live where they want," he said, "and to live the way they want to as long as they ain't hurting anybody else. Which I don't reckon you are."

"Just want to be left alone, me," she said, still not looking at him, and he wondered if somehow she had been hurt in the past. Had she left this bayou haven and ventured out into the rest of the world, gone to New Orleans maybe, and had something happen to her that was so bad she had run back here determined to spend the rest of her life among the cypresses and the bougainvillea and the water lilies?

It was none of his business, of course. After what she had done for him, he didn't want to pry too deeply into her life.

She found bowls and spoons in a wooden crate that evidently served as a pantry, then dished out the gumbo from the black iron pot on the top of the stove. Longarm sat down at the table as she brought over the food and took the chair opposite him.

"Eat up," she said with a smile. "Hope you like gumbo."

"Sure do," said Longarm. He dipped up a spoonful of the thick, steaming soup. It tasted good and was full of chopped-up okra, just the way he liked it. He said as much to Claudette, who smiled brightly.

They ate in silence for several minutes. Then Longarm asked, "How'd you happen to be down there in the marshes so that you could help me out?"

"Planned to go out into the bay and do some seinin' for shrimp, I did," she replied. She grinned across the table at him. "Caught me a big ol' fish instead."

Longarm chuckled. He had been called a lot of things in his life, but he didn't remember anyone ever referring to him as a fish before.

"A shark, maybe, with plenty-plenty sharp teeth," Claudette went on. Her smile disappeared, replaced by a solemn look. "Why you runnin' round the marshes with smuggler men tryin' to shoot you, Custis?"

Longarm hesitated, unsure how to answer that question. Claudette had an obvious antipathy for smugglers, so he didn't want to admit to working with Jasper Millard, but he wasn't just about to reveal his true identity to her either. Finally, he said vaguely, "I was on my way down to Grand Isle to see a man about a boat. Those fellas you say were smugglers jumped me for no good reason and tried to kill me." He said nothing about Millard.

Claudette nodded, seeming to accept his explanation. "Prob'ly see you and think you spyin' on 'em, they did. Hones' folks in the Delta stay away from them smugglers, you bet."

"That sounds like a good idea," said Longarm sincerely. He didn't want an innocent like Claudette getting tangled up in the feud between Millard and Royale. Of course, by helping him, she had already taken a hand, but maybe he could keep her out of any further involvement.

He scraped up the last of the gumbo, swallowed it, and asked, "What's the best way back to New Orleans from here?"

"There a road not far off. Take you there in the mornin', I can."

Longarm frowned. "I figured I'd start back to town today."

Claudette shook her head. "No. Too far to walk 'fore dark, and you don't want to be out trampin' round the bayous after the sun, she is gone down. Too many snakes, and the night is black like God damn. Best you stay here tonight, tomorrow maybe catch a ride on a wagon goin' to town."

What she said made sense, all right, but Longarm still chafed at the delay. He wanted to get back to New Orleans and find out if Millard had survived this second attack by Royale's men. Two attempts on Millard's life in less than twenty-four hours, mused Longarm. Royale was certainly turning up the heat. The friction between the two leaders of the smuggling rings was going to burst into the flame of an all-out war if this kept up.

But there was nothing he could do about it tonight, so he nodded in acceptance of Claudette's advice. "I'm much obliged," he said. "I reckon that hammock out on the front porch will hold me all right."

Again she shook her head. "You get the bunk, Custis. Gran'pere sleep there when he still alive. I take the hammock, me."

"Don't hardly seem fair," said Longarm with a frown as he reached into his pocket for a cheroot. "This is your place."

"And you my guest. Don't argue with me 'bout this, you."

He had to grin. "All right," he said as he held up his hands in mock surrender. "I'll take the bunk, and you can use the hammock."

She nodded, clearly pleased with her victory.

Nightfall was not far away now. Longarm smoked a cheroot, which Claudette said reminded her of her gran'pere's pipe. She brought out a clay jug with a wooden stopper and offered it to Longarm. "Home brew," she told him. "I like a little taste now and again, me."

"So do I," he said with a grin. He pulled the stopper with his teeth, then crooked his arm and tipped the jug to his lips. Fiery liquor flowed into his mouth. He caught his breath as the heat of it seared his gullet and fairly exploded in his belly. "Potent stuff," he said as he blew his breath back out.

"Good for the digestion." Claudette took the jug from him and downed a healthy swallow of the homemade whiskey. She wiped the back of her other hand across her mouth.

She was quite a contradiction, thought Longarm. Undeniably lovely, probably intelligent, yet she willingly lived this primitive backwoods existence . . . which, of course, was her choice and none of his business, he reminded himself. Yet he couldn't help but wonder how she would look cleaned up and in some better clothes.

Shadows were gathering outside, making it even darker in

the shack. After putting the jug away, Claudette opened the front door and said, "Good night, Custis."

"Sort of early to turn in, isn't it?"

She shrugged. "In the bayou country, not much to do after dark."

Longarm might have been able to make a suggestion or two about how they could pass the time, even in the dark, but with all Claudette had already done for him, he didn't want to force himself on her. He nodded and said, "All right then. Good night, Claudette."

She shut the door, and he heard her climb into the hammock on the front porch. Longarm went over to the bunk, trying not to think about how Claudette's grandfather had likely died there, and sat down to pull off his boots. He took off his gunbelt as well, coiling it and placing it on the floor beside the bunk within easy reach. He had already tossed his hat onto the table. That left his tie and his shirt, because he intended to keep his pants on. He undid the tie, shrugged out of the shirt, and placed both of them on the table beside his hat. The light in the room was just about gone by the time he stretched out on the bunk, feeling the ropes underneath the straw mattress sag a little.

Longarm didn't expect to go to sleep right away, but he surprised himself by dozing off almost immediately. He slept lightly, though, so he was instantly awake when he heard the soft scrape of the door opening sometime later. He was unsure exactly how much time had passed, but it was pitch dark in the cabin.

Quiet footsteps came across the room toward him. From the confidence with which the person was moving in the darkness, Longarm felt fairly sure it was Claudette. He wasn't sure why she was sneaking around like this; if she had wanted to harm him, she'd had ample opportunity before now. But he reached down and silently wrapped his fingers around the butt of his holstered Colt anyway.

He could hear her breathing as she knelt on the other side of the bed. Suddenly, something touched his chest, light as a butterfly, and he realized she was stroking him with her fingertips. She trailed her fingers through the thick dark hair that curled on his chest, moving them ever lower. She reached his waist and then moved even lower, flattening her hand to press the palm of it against the rapidly rising bulge at his groin. Through the fabric of his trousers, her fingers closed around his hardening shaft.

"Custis, I know you got to be awake," she whispered as she squeezed him lightly. "Either awake or dead, you."

"I ain't dead," he told her, his voice sounding strangely hoarse in his ears.

She squeezed harder. "Good, 'cause I need a live man tonight, me."

Longarm let go of his Colt and reached up toward her. His hand encountered soft, yielding flesh and closed around it. He could feel the pebbled ring of her nipple prodding against his palm. He squeezed her breast for a moment, then ran his thumb over the erect nub of flesh, plucking at it like a guitar string and drawing a low note of pleasure from her throat.

"Afraid you got a shameless hussy here, you bet, Custis," she said. She unbuckled his belt, and then he felt her fingers go to work on the buttons of his trousers.

"That's just fine with me," he told her, reaching up to cup her other breast.

She finished with the last button and reached inside his trousers to free his shaft. As it bobbed up, she wrapped her hand around it and began sliding her palm up and down.

"Oh, you be plenty-plenty big," she said, breathless with anticipation. "Goin' to feel so good inside me."

He slid his hands from her breasts along her flanks. As he had thought, she was naked, having shed the old dress she had been wearing earlier. He reached down and moved his hand between her thighs. He probed her with a finger, and found her hot and wet. She moaned and pressed her pelvis against him as he explored her slick femaleness.

Then she leaned over and planted a kiss on his chest. She

tongued each of his nipples for a moment, then moved down his torso, her lips and tongue leaving a fiery trail of sensation behind them. She lifted herself over him so that she could reach his manhood, and a second later, her lips closed around the tip of the throbbing pole of flesh.

Longarm's hips wanted to surge up off the bed and drive his shaft deeper into her mouth, but he controlled the urge and let Claudette set the pace. Her tongue swirled around the head and toyed with the slit at the very tip, licking up the moisture that welled from it. After a few maddening moments of that, she moved on down the shaft, kissing and licking until she had it wet all over. It was all Longarm could do not to explode in her mouth.

He caught hold of her hips and pulled her onto the bunk with him so that she lay with her thighs straddling his head. As she took his manhood into her mouth again, sucking it deeper this time, he reached down and tangled his hands in her thick dark hair. The musky scent of her femininity filled his nostrils as he lifted his head and thrust his tongue into her. She groaned around his shaft and clenched her thighs on his ears.

There was a limit to how much of this Longarm could stand without losing control, and he reached it after a few minutes. Claudette seemed to be totally willing to move on to the next step too, as he pulled her around so that she faced him. She reached down to guide the long, thick rod of flesh into her, and they were both so wet that he slid inside with no trouble. Claudette put her hands on his chest and pushed herself upright so that she was sitting on him, so stuffed with his manhood that they both felt it hit bottom. Or top, as the case might be. Claudette gasped and began to rock her hips back and forth.

"Oh, fill me up so good, you, Custis!" she cried.

He held her hips to steady her as he began thrusting up from the bunk, meeting her movements with his own. Urgency crept over him, making him drive into her harder and faster. She was caught up in the grip of passion just as he was, and she said, "Oh! . . . Oh! . . . Oh!" as he made love to her. His eyes had adjusted to the darkness inside the shack by now, and in the faint glow of moonlight and starlight that filtered through the trees and into the cabin, he could see her throwing her head back and forth, her hair whipping around it. Her fingers dug into his chest, holding on for dear life.

Finally, arching his back, Longarm drove the bar of flesh that was both velvet and iron as deeply into her as it would go, and held it there as his climax exploded from him. Spurt after spurt of the thick seed boiled from his manhood and filled her to the brim. Her own climax burst at the same time in a series of shudders that rolled through her. Longarm threw his head back and groaned through clenched teeth as the last of his juices welled out of him.

Claudette collapsed on top of him, her breasts flattening against his chest. Both of them were breathing heavily, their bodies slicked with sweat from the humid heat of the bayou country—and the heat of their lovemaking. She nuzzled her face against his shoulder for a moment. Then Longarm cupped her chin and turned her toward him so that he could kiss her. His lips brushed hers with a tenderness that might not have been possible had he not already been sated. In fact, as he tasted the sweet, hot wetness of her mouth, another throb went through his shaft, which was still buried within her. The reaction made her give a throaty little noise almost like the purr of a cat.

"I am so happy-happy I find you in that marsh, Custis," she whispered.

"You and me both, Claudette," he told her. "You and me both . . ."

Chapter 8

As Claudette had predicted, Longarm was able to hitch a ride into New Orleans the next morning with a farmer who was taking a load of produce into town to the market near the docks. That put Longarm close to Gallatin Street too, so he was able to walk to the Brass Pelican. The door of the gambling club was locked when he got there, however, so he pounded on the panel and waited to see if anyone was going to open it.

His thoughts went back to Claudette. She had awakened him that morning when dawn was just beginning to gray the sky, and a mighty nice way of waking up it had been. She had been kneeling beside the bunk, her head bobbing up and down over his groin as she sucked on his manhood. He had caught hold of her shoulder and tried to pull her up onto the bunk with him, but her lips and tongue had ceased what they were doing long enough for her to say, "No! You leave him where he is. That what I want, me."

Longarm didn't argue. He let her continue with the French lesson—appropriate enough name for it, he considered, since she was descended from those Acadian settlers who had once called France home—and after a few minutes he felt his climax nearing again. Claudette seemed to sense it too, because she gripped his stalk firmly with one hand and tightened her lips around it, as if to make sure that he didn't get away from her.

That was the last thing he had in mind. He poured out his seed into her mouth as she swallowed eagerly. She had reached down between her legs to rub herself, and her hips were pumping back and forth in a frenzy as she drained him, using her hand to squeeze out the last drops so that she could lap them up. Longarm flopped back on the bunk and reflected that if he didn't get back to New Orleans pretty soon, this lusty Cajun gal was liable to just about love him to death.

After that she fed him breakfast, showed him the road she had mentioned the night before, and gave him a sweet kiss of farewell. He had walked along the road only about a mile when a farmer came along with a wagon loaded with produce, and now here he was standing in front of the Brass Pelican, lifting his hand to knock once more on the door.

Before he could do so, the panel swung open, and a man with a narrow, pasty face peered out at him, blinking from the midmorning glare. The man looked like the sort who didn't often actually see the sun. Longarm recognized him as one of the bartenders he had seen in the club a couple of nights earlier.

"Yeah?" growled the man. "What the hell do you want?"

"You must not recognize me, old son." Longarm put his shoulder against the door and easily shoved it open, stepping inside as the bartender stumbled back a couple of steps. "Is Millard here?"

"Mr. Millard!" yelled the man as he reached behind him to jerk something from behind his belt. Longarm was expecting the little pistol he saw in the bartender's hand, and he reached out to close his own hand over the cylinder so that the gun couldn't fire. With a quick wrench, Longarm plucked the pistol from the bartender's fingers, twisting one of them in the process. The man yelped and jumped back again, sticking the injured digit in his mouth to suck on it.

Jasper Millard appeared in the doorway at the end of the bar, a shotgun in his hands. He had the greener cocked and ready for trouble, no doubt thinking that Royale might be staging another attack on the club. Longarm held up his hand, palm out, and said hurriedly, "Hold on, Mr. Millard. It's just me, Custis Parker."

"Parker!" exclaimed Millard in surprise. He pointed the double barrels of the greener at the floor and carefully lowered the hammers. "Damn it, I didn't expect to see you again. I was afraid that if Royale's men didn't get you, the swamp would."

Longarm shook his head. He tossed the pocket pistol back to the bartender, who glared at him even though it was obvious Longarm wasn't one of the enemy. Longarm ignored the man and strolled along the bar to join Millard.

"Reckon I was lucky. I see you were too."

"I know my way around those marshes. I grew up down there."

"You don't sound like a Cajun," Longarm pointed out.

Millard shrugged his brawny shoulders. "I was gone for a long time before I came back to New Orleans. Suppose I lost the accent somewhere along the way. But I never forgot how easy it is to bring in goods through the Delta." He turned and inclined his head to indicate that Longarm was to follow him. "Let's go back to the office."

Longarm followed the bald-headed man down the hall, and once they were in the office, Millard waved at the chair in front of the desk. Longarm sat down and cocked his right ankle on his left knee. He was still wearing the mud-stained clothes he had worn the day before.

"You look like you've been through the wringer," said Millard as he sat down behind the desk. "Help yourself to one of those cigars." He nodded toward the humidor.

Longarm reached into his pocket for a cheroot. "Reckon I'll smoke my own."

Millard frowned across the desk at him. "What's the matter, Parker?" he asked. "You're acting like somebody shoved a burr up your ass."

Longarm flicked a lucifer into life with an iron-hard thumbnail and held the flame to the end of his cheroot. When he had it burning to suit him, he shook the match out and dropped it on the floor beside the chair. "You sort of disappeared yesterday after we ran into Royale's boys."

The frown on Millard's face deepened. "What the hell is this?" he snapped. "You're mad because I didn't stay around to pull your fat out of the fire?"

"I got the notion we were working together."

"Well, you got the wrong notion!" Millard said with a snort. "You're working for me, Parker. We ain't partners." His eyes narrowed. "I warned you about getting too ambitious."

Longarm sighed. He had pushed this mock resentment about as far as he was going to. But he had figured that a man as tough and amoral as he was supposed to be ought to say *something* about being left behind to face a pack of vicious killers.

"You're right, Boss," he muttered. "Sorry. To tell you the truth, I'm just glad we both got out of there with our hides in one piece."

Millard grunted, seeming to accept Longarm's apology. "Yeah, so am I. The way things are going, I expect Royale to pull something else any time now."

"Maybe since his boys failed the last couple of times, he'll think twice about starting more trouble."

Millard shook his head. "I'd like to think so, but I doubt it. I got a feeling Royale's not going to let up until either him or me is dead." He looked curiously at Longarm. "How'd you get away from his men anyway?"

"Pure dumb luck," said Longarm with a grin. He wasn't going to mention Claudette. "My horse got sucked down by quicksand, and I knew I couldn't take off across those marshes on foot without winding up the same way. But I found an old pirogue and started paddling around those bayous, and that kept me from getting sucked under. Royale's men were hollering at each other while they looked for us, so I just steered clear of them as much as I could. Didn't hear any more shots, so I was hoping you'd gotten away too.''

"How did you get back here to New Orleans?''

Longarm puffed on his cheroot, then blew out the smoke and said, "First I found me a tree to climb up into so I wouldn't have to spend the night on the ground. Then when the sun came up this morning, I paddled on some more until I came across a road. Figured it had to lead me back to town sooner or later, so I started walking. Wasn't long before a farmer came along heading to market and gave me a ride on his wagon. Fella brought me practically right to your door.''

As stories went, it was a little far-fetched, Longarm knew, but it was certainly possible that everything could have happened that way. And Millard had no reason to doubt him either. In fact, the club owner began nodding his bald head even as Longarm finished the concoction of lies and half-truths.

"You're lucky, all right,'' said Millard. "Damn lucky. Fella like you who doesn't know the bayou country ought to be in some gator's belly after spending a night out in the open like that.''

The mention of alligators reminded Longarm of Douglas Ramsey. He shuddered and said, "Don't talk about gators. I never have liked those critters.''

A humorless grin plucked at Millard's mouth. "They come in handy sometimes,'' he said cryptically.

Longarm kept the reaction he felt hidden, but his heart began to slug a little harder. Was Millard talking about how Marshal Ramsey's body had been disposed of? Or did he have something else in mind? Given the line of work Millard was in, he might have had plenty of *other* bodies to get rid of. Millard's comment still wasn't the proof Longarm needed to feel certain he was responsible for Ramsey's death.

But there was another angle Longarm had yet to explore. Maybe it was time for that, he thought.

"What do you intend to do about Royale?" he asked. "Reckon you could put one of those voodoo curses or something like that on him?"

Millard frowned again. "What do you mean by that?" he demanded.

"I thought everybody in New Orleans did that voodoo stuff," said Longarm with an innocent shrug. "Sticking pins in dolls, things like that."

From the way Millard was glaring, even the mention of voodoo was a sore point with him. "Nobody in his right mind messes with voodoo. It's too easy to get the people who believe in it all stirred up." He paused, then added, "Anyway, only a fool would really believe in that mumbo jumbo."

"Reckon you're right," Longarm said easily, appearing to forget about the subject entirely as he went on. "What happened with that shipment of goods you went down to the Delta to set up yesterday?"

"Royale's men killed several of the Cajuns who work for me," replied Millard, his face still grim. "But I'm going to get those goods anyway. I sent a dozen well-armed men down there this morning to collect them. Would've sent you with them, Parker—if I'd known you were still alive."

Longarm shrugged. "I was still trying to get back to town. Sorry I let you down, Boss. I should've been able to do something about that ambush yesterday."

"There wasn't anything you could have done," Millard said with a shake of his head. "The odds were too heavy against us. I didn't expect Royale to go to that much trouble so soon after his men raided the club." Millard's dark eyes narrowed ominously. "Looks like I'm going to have to take a good-sized group of men with me wherever I go for a while, till things settle down again."

Longarm wasn't sure things were going to settle down. Royale seemed to be dead set on bringing the rivalry between him and Millard to an end, one way or the other. Longarm kept that thought to himself, however. As long as Millard was having trouble, he would need Longarm around—and that was just what Longarm wanted.

"You might as well go on back to your hotel and get cleaned up," continued Millard. "You could probably use some real sleep too, after spending the night in a tree."

"I *am* a mite tired," admitted Longarm, although in truth he had slept just fine between bouts of lovemaking with Claudette. "Don't you need me to stay here, though?"

Millard shook his head. "I don't plan to leave the club today, and I'm safe enough here."

"Couldn't prove it by the fella who let me in," Longarm pointed out. "If I'd been working for Royale, you might be dead now."

"Maybe you're right," said Millard. "But I've got more men upstairs. I'll roust them out and put a couple of guards with shotguns on every entrance."

"Wouldn't hurt to have a couple of them right out there in the hall, in front of your door."

"Good idea." Millard stood up. "I'll see to it right now. Why don't you come back over here after supper?"

Longarm nodded. "All right. If you're sure . . ."

"I'm sure. Go on, Parker."

Longarm left the club, hoping that Millard would follow through on those precautions they had discussed. To tell the truth, he really was tired, and he wanted to get out of his dirty clothes. A hot bath, a few hours' sleep, and a fresh outfit would go a long way toward making him feel like a new man.

He hailed one of the hansom cabs and headed for the St. Charles Hotel.

By the time he returned to the Brass Pelican that evening, he did indeed feel positively human again. Well rested, dressed in a clean suit and shirt, he felt as if his adventure in the bayou country was now nothing more than a memory.

But a sweet memory in a lot of ways, he thought as an image of Claudette floated in his mind for a moment.

Now it was time for him to get back to work. There was a new doorman at the entrance of the Brass Pelican, replacing the unfortunate Luther. This man wore a fancy uniform too, but since he was about half Luther's size, Longarm knew it wasn't the same outfit.

The club was busy, though not as packed as it had been two nights earlier before the raid by Royale's men. Such an incident would hurt Millard's business for a time, before everyone forgot about it. Royale might not allow anyone to forget what had happened, thought Longarm. There might be a recurrence at any time.

Paul Clement was bucking the tiger at the faro table tonight, and as usual, his sister Annie was at his side. Her face lit up in a smile as she saw Longarm making his way across the room toward them. "Look, Paul," Longarm heard her say as she clutched at her brother's arm. "It's Custis."

"So it is," said Clement as he looked up with his customary sardonic half-smile. He greeted Longarm by saying, "How are you, Custis? Annie here was quite worried about you last night. She expected to see you here again. She's been pestering Jasper about you all evening."

Annie blushed and looked down at the floor. "Really, Paul, you make it sound as if I was being silly," she protested. "Last night, I simply asked Mr. Millard where Custis was, and I've barely spoken to him this evening."

"What did Millard tell you?" asked Longarm.

"He said that you were handling some business for him, and that he hoped you'd be back tonight." Annie smiled again. "And here you are!" She sounded a little giddy, and Longarm suspected she'd had several glasses of wine.

"I'm sorry I missed you," he said, only half-sincere. The run-in with Royale's men hadn't been any fun, but it had led to his meeting with Claudette.

"Well, you're here now," said Annie, disengaging her arm from her brother's and linking it with Longarm's instead. Longarm thought he saw a flicker of disapproval on Clement's face, but he couldn't be sure about that. He knew that Clement regarded Annie as a lucky charm. She went on. "Why don't we get a drink?"

"Sure . . . if it's all right with Paul."

Clement flicked his wrist languidly. "Go ahead. I'm afraid not even the good luck Annie sometimes brings me could make me a winner tonight."

Longarm led Annie over to the bar. She chattered brightly in his ear along the way, but he didn't pay much attention to what she was saying. His eyes roved the room, searching for any sign of trouble, but everything seemed to be normal in the Brass Pelican tonight. He spotted Jasper Millard in his customary spot at the end of the bar. The club owner nodded to Longarm, smiling slightly. He wondered just how much of a pest Annie Clement had made of herself.

Annie drank several glasses of wine over the next couple of hours, and combined with what she had had before, it had quite an effect on her. Longarm had never cared for drunken women, but instead of getting sloppy and maudlin, Annie seemed to grow brighter and more animated the more she drank. She laughed merrily no matter what Longarm said to her. When she finally began to sway too much, he sat her down at one of the tables and continued to nurse his own drink, which was only his second. He wanted to stay clear-headed in case of trouble.

His thoughts never strayed far from the case that had brought him here. Earlier in the day, Millard had made that comment about alligators, but he had also responded with fervent disapproval to Longarm's question about voodoo. If Millard had been telling the truth about the way he felt, it was unlikely he had been responsible for leaving that half-doll on the doorstep of the chief marshal's office. He seemed not to want to have anything to do with such things, and he had scoffed at anybody who believed in them.

But had that ridicule been intended merely to cover up the

man's own very real fear of voodoo? Longarm wondered. That was entirely possible.

Paul Clement wandered over and sat down at the table with them, sighing. "Ah, well, cleaned out again," he said. "I allow myself to lose only a certain amount on each night of our visits to New Orleans, and tonight I have reached my limit."

"Too bad," said Longarm. He glanced over at Annie, saw that she was looking off at the other side of the room and humming to herself, then added quietly, "I reckon your sister has just about reached her limit too."

Clement's mouth tightened. "Annie, have you had too much to drink again?"

She opened her mouth and stared at him for a moment before saying, "Paul, whatever do you mean? Custis and I have been having the most wonderful time—"

"You know that you don't feel well later on when you drink too much," said Clement, his attitude a mixture of solicitousness and impatience. "Why don't I take you home—"

"No!" exclaimed Annie. "I want Custis to take me home."

"I don't think that's a good idea." Clement glanced at Longarm. "No offense, Custis."

"None taken," Longarm assured him with a slight shake of his head.

"Custis will take me home," insisted Annie, "and he will take me upstairs, and then he—"

"That's *enough*, Annie." The hard edge of menace in Clement's tone made his sister fall silent. He reached across the table and took her hand. "Come along now."

Her lovely features set in a sullen pout, Annie allowed her brother to tug her to her feet. "G'night, Custis," she said, turning to Longarm. "Some other night . . ."

"Sure," he said. Truth be told, he doubted if he would enjoy bedding Annie tonight. As much as she'd had to drink, she likely wouldn't remember anything in the morning, and she would also be liable to fall asleep and start snoring right in the middle of the festivities.

Clement led her out of the club. She was still only a little unsteady on her feet. The lady had quite a capacity, Longarm reflected, but as he had warned Clement, she had definitely reached her limits.

Millard came over to the table and took the seat Paul Clement had vacated. "Looked like Mademoiselle Annie had a little too much to drink," he said.

"Does she do that often?" Longarm asked curtly.

Millard shrugged. "I've only seen her that way once or twice. She was really shook up by you not being here last night." He grinned. "You'd better enjoy the lady while you've got the chance, Parker. Her brother keeps her on a pretty tight rein most of the time."

That was probably a good idea, thought Longarm. He changed the subject by saying, "Doesn't look like Royale is going to try anything tonight."

Millard was instantly serious again. "I don't know," he said dubiously. "After the past couple of days, I'll believe it when I see it."

In fact, the rest of the evening passed peacefully in the Brass Pelican. Not quietly, reflected Longarm, not with all the music and laughter, the clicking of poker chips and the roulette wheel, but definitely peacefully. The crowd began to thin out as the hours past midnight rolled by. At four o'clock, there were only a few persistent drinkers and gamblers in the place, and Longarm was starting to yawn.

He was leaning on the bar when Millard came over to him and said, "You might as well head back to your room, Parker. We'll be closing down in a few minutes."

"Wasn't sure a place like this ever closed," commented Longarm.

"Yeah, we lock up for a while. Gives the boys a chance to get a little sleep."

"Well, I'll stay until you're ready to call it a night," Longarm said. "Just in case Royale's trying to lull us into thinking we've made it through without any trouble.''

Millard nodded, obviously understanding Longarm's point. Over the next half hour, though, as the last of the Brass Pelican's patrons were gradually eased out of the place, nothing unusual happened. Longarm was the last person out the door.

"No need for you to be back here until this evening," Millard told him.

"You're not planning any more trips down to the bayou country?"

Millard shook his head. "Not for a few more days. I'll let you know ahead of time, don't worry."

"All right," Longarm said with a nod. "See you tonight, Boss."

The door closed behind him, and Longarm heard the key turn in the lock. Behind the thick walls of the club, protected by well-armed guards, Millard ought to be safe enough.

The only way to get at him now, thought Longarm with a grin, was with some of that voodoo. . . .

He chuckled tiredly to himself as he looked around for a cab. There were none to be seen. The customers who had departed recently had probably engaged all the cabs that normally hung around the outside of the club. Longarm grunted. Looked like he might have to walk back to the St. Charles. Well, it wasn't really all that far, he told himself.

Gallatin Street had calmed down a little due to the late hour, but it was still a busy place. Quite a few people were on the sidewalks, and Longarm kept a close eye on them as he strolled along. This was the sort of neighborhood where a fella could get his throat cut for his pocket watch—or even less. He remembered what Millard had said about how his friends and associates were safe in Gallatin Street, but that only applied if the would-be cutthroat knew that his intended victim was connected with Millard. Anybody could make a mistake.

No one bothered Longarm, however. People seemed to be minding their own business. A couple of whores tried to entice him into their cribs, but he just grinned, tipped his hat, and walked on.

Still, despite the lack of anything suspicious, Longarm felt the hair on the back of his neck beginning to rise. His years as a lawman had given him a finely honed instinct for trouble. Sometimes he thought it bordered on the downright supernatural, and he had learned to trust it. He glanced over his shoulder, saw nothing unusual, and walked on.

Gallatin Street merged with Decatur, and as Longarm left the notorious district behind, the city blocks became darker and more deserted. He could still hear music in the night and an occasional burst of laughter, but he was soon the only pedestrian in sight. His footsteps echoed hollowly against the walls of the buildings he passed.

Then, as if to confirm that his instincts were still true, the scrape of soft, dragging footsteps came from somewhere behind him.

Longarm's muscles tensed at the sound, but he kept walking, not wanting to betray by his actions that he had heard it. It was possible, of course, that whoever was walking back there had nothing at all to do with him.

Possible . . . but every nerve in his body was screaming that that was not the case.

Whoever it was didn't seem to be in any hurry. Longarm kept his own pace casual, deliberate. He passed underneath one of the gas street lamps of which the city fathers were so proud, walked on half a block, then glanced over his shoulder. He caught just a glimpse of a figure passing out of the circle of illumination. A big man, dressed in rough work clothing. A stevedore from the docks, maybe. Just somebody on his way to work, Longarm told himself. Dawn was not far off, and dock workers started their day early.

The only problem with that theory was that the docks were in the other direction.

By now, Royale had to have figured out that Longarm was working for Jasper Millard. Royale's men would have seen him twice, once saving Millard from the bushwhack attempt during the raid on the club and again during the ambush down in the bayou country. They probably had a pretty good idea that he was Millard's new right-hand man. That would give Royale a good reason for wanting him dead—or better yet, a prisoner who could be interrogated and made to give up all of Millard's secrets.

As a point of fact, Longarm didn't really *know* any of Millard's secrets just yet. But Royale might not be aware of that.

Whether Royale wanted him killed or captured didn't really matter. Longarm didn't intend to allow either of those things to come to pass.

He walked under another street light, still taking it slow and easy. From the sound of the footsteps behind him, the fella who was shuffling along back there had closed up the gap a little. But he wasn't in any hurry either. He sure did drag his feet too, noted Longarm. The footsteps were slow but inexorable, and they came steadily closer.

Longarm glanced back again, and this time he got a better look at his follower. The man was so tall and broad-shouldered that he reminded Longarm of a medium-sized tree. His arms hung limply at his sides and seemed to dangle almost to his knees. His dark, curly hair was cut short, and in the light of the street lamp, his skin was like rich chocolate.

Why would some gigantic black fella be following him? Longarm wondered. The man wasn't wearing a derby and a bandanna mask, and he didn't strike Longarm as the type that Royale would have hired in the first place. All the rest of Royale's paid killers had been white.

Longarm reached a corner and turned, not even noticing what street he was on. He just wanted to give the slip to the man trailing him, then turn the tables and do a little trailing of his own. His two looks back should have given the big black man the idea that he realized he was being followed. Now Longarm ducked into the first alley mouth he found, letting the shadows swallow him. He waited for the slap-slap of running footsteps as the man hurried to catch up to him.

Instead, the slow shuffle continued. Longarm had no trouble knowing where the man was just by listening. The man reached the corner and rounded it, coming steadily toward the alley where Longarm was hidden. The lawman waited, drawing his Colt as the steps came nearer.

But instead of stopping, the man plodded right past the darkened mouth of the alley. Longarm saw him, a huge patch of deeper darkness in the shadows that cloaked the street.

The man continued for several steps, and as he did Longarm wondered if he had been completely mistaken about being followed. From the looks of it, the man didn't have any interest in him at all.

But then the man stopped short, as if drawn up at the end of a rope. He stood there for a long moment, just past the alley mouth, and then slowly, ponderously, he began to turn around. He moved toward the alley, lifting his arms as he came. The fingers on the hamlike hands spread out, as if ready to wrap themselves around somebody's neck.

Longarm was certain now just whose neck the fella was after.

He stepped out of the alley before the man could get there, raising his gun and pointing it toward the giant, menacing shape. "Hold it right there, old son," Longarm said. "I don't know what business you got with me, but I reckon we can talk it over."

He thought there was still plenty of room between them, but he hadn't counted on the man being able to cover that distance in one huge step. The man lurched forward, reaching out with those long fingers. There was a certain awkwardness about his movements, but he was quick enough.

Almost quick enough anyway. Longarm twisted aside so that the giant stumbled past him. "Damn it!" Longarm snapped in frustration. He didn't want to have to kill the man. A corpse couldn't answer any questions.

The giant caught himself and swung around, lashing out with an arm and trying to backhand Longarm. Longarm ducked underneath the blow, letting it pass harmlessly over his head. Once the man started something, he seemed unable to stop until he had completed the action, whatever it was. Maybe he was a mite slow in the head, thought Longarm. The expression on the man's face when he passed beneath that second street lamp had been rather dull, and the threat of Longarm's gun seemed utterly meaningless to him.

Longarm danced back along the sidewalk, putting himself out of reach again. "Blast it, old son," he grated, "I'm going to have to put a bullet in your knee if you don't settle down. You won't ever walk right again if I do that."

The man made no response except to lurch toward Longarm again. In fact, Longarm realized as a cold touch rippled up his spine, the man hadn't made a sound during the entire encounter. Longarm hadn't heard anything from him except the shuffle and scrape of his shoes on the cobblestones. The fella wasn't even breathing heavy.

The coldness along Longarm's spine got even icier as he realized that he couldn't tell if the man was breathing at all.

He shoved that thought out of his mind and darted aside, avoiding the giant's lunge once more. This time, however, the man seemed more prepared for Longarm's response. He reached back, even as he was stumbling to a halt, and caught hold of Longarm's coat sleeve.

The man's strength was like nothing Longarm had ever faced before. He found himself literally jerked off his feet and swung around. His back slammed into the wall of a building, knocking the air out of his lungs and the hat off his head. As he bounced off the wall, the giant's other hand clamped onto his throat.

Caught like that with no air in his body, Longarm felt the desperation of a dying man almost as soon as the fingers closed around his throat in a grip like iron. His vision turned red and muddy, and he could barely make out the huge shape looming right in front of him. He slashed at where he thought the man's head was with the barrel of the Colt and felt it strike something soft and yielding. Almost in a frenzy, Long-

88

arm lashed out again and again, pistol-whipping the man who was trying to kill him.

The fingers locked around his throat didn't budge.

The fight continued in eerie silence. Longarm's feet were off the ground. The giant pressed him back against the brick wall of the building, supporting him with that dreadful grip around his throat. Longarm felt his strength ebbing away, and couldn't lift the gun to hit the man again. The part of his brain that was still working told him he was going to pass out in a matter of seconds, and if he did, he knew he would never wake up this side of the grave.

There was only one thing he could do, while he still had a little strength.

He jammed the barrel of the gun against the body of his attacker and started pulling the trigger.

The massive body muffled the roar of the shots to a certain extent, but they were still so deafening to Longarm that they almost drowned out the insane pounding of blood in his head. He emptied the Colt of all five shots and wished he had loaded the empty chamber for a change, rather than letting the hammer rest on it. For a horrible moment, he thought that the bullets hadn't had any effect, because the giant kept choking the life out of him.

How can you kill something that's already dead?

He forced that thought out of his mind as he felt a slight lessening of the pressure on his windpipe. Maybe it was just his imagination, maybe just wishful thinking, but he wasn't going to let it pass. He dropped the empty gun, grabbed the giant's arm with both hands, and wrenched with every bit of strength left in his body.

The fingers slipped off his throat.

Longarm shoved the giant's arm away and heaved great, gasping breaths into his body, filling his lungs. He slid along the wall of the building, out of the giant's reach. He was in such bad shape that if the man came after him again, he wouldn't even be able to put up a fight.

But the giant wasn't coming after him. In the dim light

from the street lamps on Decatur, Longarm saw that the man was swaying back and forth, and then he began to slowly topple backward, reminding Longarm once again of a tree. Still without making a sound, he crashed to the cobblestones and lay motionless, arms and legs spraddled out.

Longarm's head was still spinning, but he knew he couldn't wait for the world to settle down in front of his eyes. He stumbled forward, bent over, and fumbled around on the street until he found his gun. He scooped it up and backed quickly away from the fallen giant, putting his back against the wall of the building once more so that nothing else could come at him out of the dark. Moving as much by instinct as by design, he dumped the empty brass from the cylinder of the Colt and thumbed in fresh cartridges that he took from his coat pocket.

Only when the gun was fully loaded did he approach the dead man again. The fella had to be dead, Longarm told himself. He had five slugs in him, enough to kill anybody. But those shots should have dropped him immediately, and it had taken him forever to go down. At least it had seemed like forever to Longarm.

Longarm was ready to pump five more bullets into him if necessary, though. He wanted a better look at this man who had almost killed him. Somebody had probably reported those shots, and the New Orleans police would be here soon.

With the gun held ready in his right hand, Longarm used his left to fish out a lucifer. He bent over and struck the match on the rough surface of the street. It flared up with a stink of sulphur—

Which made sense, thought Longarm, because he had surely descended into the fiery pits of Hades. Either that or gone mad, because staring up at him was the face of Luther.

Luther, the former doorman at the Brass Pelican. Luther, who had been murdered two nights earlier by Royale's men.

Longarm had almost had the life choked out of him by a walking dead man.

Chapter 9

For a moment, there was a part of Longarm that wanted to drop the match and run like hell. He knew now why Billy Vail had asked him if he was superstitious. The voodoo angle to this case had sort of faded into the background as Longarm got caught up in investigating the rival smuggling rings headed by Jasper Millard and the mysterious Royale.

But it had just poked its ugly head into things again, sure enough, because Longarm was staring down in horror at an honest-to-God *zombie*.

Or was he?

The rational part of Longarm's brain began to reassert itself. He recalled how Luther had stumbled into the Brass Pelican, gutshot by Royale's men. The body sprawled on its back in the street had a huge bloodstain on its midsection where Longarm had emptied the Colt into it. That matched Luther's stomach wound, of course, but how could a man who had been dead for over forty-eight hours bleed that much?

But then, how could a man who had been dead for over forty-eight hours be wandering around the streets of New

Orleans and trying to murder federal lawmen? Longarm gave a little shake of his head, trying to keep his mind from wandering too far off down dark paths.

Quickly, before the match went out, Longarm holstered his gun and reached down to grasp the dead man's shoulder. There was one sure test. He had seen Luther shot at nearly point-blank range in the back of the head by one of Royale's men. With a grunt of effort, Longarm heaved the massive corpse onto its side. He held the match closer to the back of the dead man's skull.

There was no bullet hole, no sign of a wound of any kind. With a sigh of relief, Longarm let go of the body and let it slump onto its back again.

So this dead man wasn't Luther after all. He just looked a hell of a lot like the doorman from the Brass Pelican.

Which still didn't answer the question of why he had been trying to kill Longarm . . . or why he had shuffled along the way he had . . . or why he had fought in complete silence and stood up for so long against the impact of five slugs from a .44.

Zombie. The word echoed in Longarm's brain.

Grimacing, he shook out the match just before it could burn his fingers and backed away from the body. He turned around and found his hat, picking it up and putting it on as he walked quickly along the street. He headed away from Decatur Street and soon found himself on Chartres Street. The mansion where Annie and Paul Clement lived when they were visiting New Orleans wasn't far from where he was, he realized. He wondered how they would react if he knocked on their door in the cold gray light of dawn and told them he'd just had a run-in with a walking dead man. They'd probably try to have him locked up in an asylum somewhere.

Maybe that was where he belonged. He had always been a rational, pragmatic, even hardheaded man. Carrying a badge made a fella that way. Now here he was thinking all sorts of wild thoughts, considering possibilities that he never would have dreamed he would consider.

There had to be an explanation. There just *had* to be.

But as he made his way back to the St. Charles Hotel by a roundabout route, he was damned if he could think of what it might be.

He slept the sleep of exhaustion—slept like a dead man, he told himself wryly when he woke up in the middle of the afternoon—but he didn't feel particularly rested. When he showed up at the Brass Pelican after a meal and several cups of strong black coffee, he felt a little better, but the bartender who was working behind the mahogany took one look at him and said, "Lord, you look like death warmed over, Mr. Parker."

Longarm rubbed his jaw and said hoarsely, "Didn't figure I looked that good."

"You coming down with the grippe? I can fix up a tonic for that."

Longarm shook his head. "No, I just . . . strained my throat, I reckon you could say. It's getting better, but thanks anyway."

"Well, if you change your mind, just let me know."

This fella was a lot friendlier than the one who had unlocked the door for Longarm the day before. Of course, the club was open for business now, so that might have had something to do with his helpful attitude. Longarm looked around the big room. There were quite a few customers drinking and gambling, though not nearly as many as there would be later.

He turned back to the bar and said, "I could use a cup of coffee. And put a dollop of Tom Moore in it."

"Coming right up, Mr. Parker."

When he had first gotten up, Longarm had barely been able to talk at all, and swallowing had been hell. But the muscles in his bruised throat had loosened up, and hot coffee seemed to help the soreness. He was only a little hoarse now, and the discomfort was tolerable. It could have been a lot worse.

He could have been dead, like that poor son of a bitch he'd had to shoot.

The more he thought about it, the more he wondered if the fella had been drugged. In the horror of the night before, Longarm hadn't really considered that possibility. It made more sense than believing in voodoo and zombies, though. Longarm recalled seeing Chinese hatchet men who had smoked so much opium that they might not have noticed right away if somebody emptied a Colt into their bellies.

Maybe Royale *had* sent the gigantic black man after him. Maybe that was just a new weapon in the war against Millard and anybody who worked for him.

Longarm sipped the coffee the bartender brought to him, feeling the bracing effect of the Maryland rye that had been added to it. He turned to the man and asked, "Where's Mr. Millard? Back in the office?"

The bartender took out his watch and glanced at it. "He's probably upstairs. He usually takes one of the girls up to his room about this time of day, if you know what I mean."

Longarm did indeed. Some men liked their loving on a regular schedule.

Carrying the coffee cup, Longarm wandered around the room, watching the players at the poker tables, the blackjack tables, the roulette wheel, and the faro bank. Not a lot of money was changing hands. The really big players, like Paul Clement, usually showed up at night. For a while, he sat down at an empty table and sipped the rest of the coffee, then got up and walked rather aimlessly toward the door that led to the rear hallway. No one challenged him as he slipped through it and headed for Millard's office.

He hoped that Millard was also a man who liked to take his time when bedding a woman, because Longarm intended to have a look in the office and see what he could find.

The corridor was empty. Longarm checked the knob of the office door, and found it unlocked. He rapped lightly on the panel, and when he got no response, opened the door silently and stepped into the office.

The lamp on Millard's desk was turned down low, but it was lit. Longarm didn't know if that meant Millard would be back soon or not. He eased the door shut behind him, then stepped quickly to the desk. Unless he knew better, he was going to assume there was no time to waste.

Longarm had searched desks before, and he made fast work of this one. He found nothing unusual at first, just the typical paperwork that went with any legitimate business. And for New Orleans, the Brass Pelican *was* a legitimate business. It was Millard's smuggling activities that put him on the wrong side of the law.

Longarm also found a couple of pistols, a Bowie knife, a bottle of cognac like the one he had shared with Millard and the Clements on his first night in the Crescent City, and a smaller bottle of dark brown glass. It had a cork stopper in its neck, and when Longarm pulled it and took a sniff, he recognized the heavy, sweetish smell of laudanum. With a grimace, he replaced the cork and put the bottle back in the drawer where he had found it.

Whatever drug that giant had been full of, it was even stronger than laudanum, thought Longarm.

Under a litter of old lottery tickets in the last drawer he checked, he found a small notebook. Flipping it open, he saw that someone, no doubt Millard, had used it to keep track of shipping activities. The names of ships, departure dates, and destinations had all been written down in a scrawling, looping hand. Longarm turned to the last page where entries had been made. Four ships were listed there, and the date of their departure had been one day before Longarm arrived in New Orleans.

Their destination was listed as Saint Laurent.

Longarm frowned. Saint Laurent was the West Indian island where Annie and Paul Clement lived most of the year, where they had their ancestral sugar plantation. Though Longarm hadn't run across any evidence linking them with

Millard's smuggling operation, he could conceive of Millard and Paul Clement joining forces to bring in shiploads of contraband sugar. From what he had seen and heard so far, however, Clement paid the import fees and sold his sugar on the exchange, all open and aboveboard.

Maybe Millard and Clement were smuggling in something else, although for the life of him, Longarm couldn't figure out what it might be. Or maybe Millard was smuggling something *into* Saint Laurent for the Clements, but again, Longarm had no idea what. And it was always possible that the ships bound for the West Indies had nothing to do with Annie and her brother at all.

Longarm knew he would have to ponder those questions later, maybe do a little poking around down on the docks. For now, he closed the notebook and replaced it under the lottery tickets where he had found it.

Just in time too, because he heard footsteps in the hall and Millard's voice. By the time the club owner opened the door and stepped into the room, Longarm was lounging in the chair in front of the desk, right foot cocked on left knee, one of the Cuban cigars smoldering in his fingers. He looked up and around at Millard, who had stopped short just inside the door, and put a slightly sheepish grin on his face. "Aw, hell," said Longarm, "you caught me."

"What are you doing in here, Parker?" Millard asked sharply.

Longarm gestured with the cigar. "I got a hankering for another of these fancy see-gars of yours, Boss. Didn't think you'd mind if I helped myself to one."

"Well, you thought wrong," snapped Millard. "I don't like people poking around my office."

Well, then, old son, you ought to keep it locked, thought Longarm, but he said, "I'm sorry, Mr. Millard. I didn't mean no harm."

Millard came around behind the desk and sat down. "Don't let it happen again," he grunted as his gaze quickly darted around the top of the desk. Longarm knew he was checking to see if anything had been disturbed. Millard wouldn't be able to tell by looking that the desk had been searched. Longarm was too good at his job for that; everything had been put back exactly the way he'd found it.

"Any sign of trouble from Royale today?" asked Longarm, partly out of curiosity, partly to distract Millard from finding him in here.

Millard shook his bald head. "It's been quiet. Maybe too quiet."

That was a suspicious nature working on Millard, thought Longarm. After everything that had happened, he would spook pretty easily. Longarm told himself to remember that; it might come in handy later on.

In the meantime, he was wondering about something else. In a tone calculated to seem only idly curious, he said, "That fella Luther who was your doorman, the one who was killed by Royale's men that first night . . . did he have a brother?"

Millard looked at him with a confused frown. "Not that I know of," he said. "Why do you ask?"

"Well . . . you might think this is a little strange . . . but I would have sworn I saw Luther on the street last night when I was going home." Longarm didn't say anything about being followed, or the fight with the massive black man, or the fact that for a few harrowing moments, it had seemed like even bullets weren't enough to take down the man.

Millard stared at him for a second, then clenched a fist and brought it down hard on the desk. "Shit!" he exploded. "I knew better . . . I knew we shouldn't—"

Longarm sensed that he was on the verge of something important here, and it was all he could do not to lean forward eagerly. All he could do was allow himself to appear mildly surprised by Millard's reaction. "What's the matter, Boss?" he asked. "Did I say something wrong?"

"No, damn it, it's just . . . Are you sure you saw Luther?"

Longarm looked perplexed. "Why, how could I do that? He's dead. I just figured I saw somebody who looked a whole lot like him. That's why I asked you if he had a brother.''

"I don't know," Millard said with a shake of his head. "Could be, could be. I suppose that has to be the explanation." He didn't sound completely convinced of that, however.

Longarm forced a chuckle. "The only other thing I could think of was that maybe Luther had been turned into one of those, what you call 'em, zombies or something. After all, this *is* New Orleans."

The comment provoked a reaction from Millard, just as Longarm had thought it might. Once again the man thumped his fist on the desk and said tautly, "Forget it. That's all just a bunch of made-up mumbo jumbo, and I don't want to hear another damn word about it, understand?" His voice rose as he spoke.

"Sure, Boss, sure," murmured Longarm. He was convinced now that Millard was scared to death of the very idea of voodoo and zombies and such. That meant he was unlikely to have been the one who'd planted the mutilated doll representing Douglas Ramsey on the chief marshal's doorstep.

But that still left Royale.

Longarm went on. "I've been thinking that if we could get a line on Royale, maybe find out who he is—"

"I've tried," Millard broke in. "Lord knows, I've tried. Nobody seems to be able to touch him."

Before Longarm could continue the discussion, there was a soft knock on the office door. At a gesture from Millard, Longarm got up and moved to the side of the door. With all the trouble that had been going on lately, it paid to be cautious. He drew his gun and called, "Yeah?"

The voice of the bartender Longarm had spoken to earlier said, "That you, Mr. Parker? You're the one I need to see, and I thought you might be in there with the boss."

Longarm opened the door a crack and saw the man standing in the corridor alone. No one was forcing him to say anything at gunpoint. Longarm hadn't really expected that to be the case, but it didn't hurt to be sure.

"What is it?" asked Longarm.

"There's somebody out here looking for you, Mr. Parker," replied the bartender. "She says you know her."

"Miss Clement?"

The bartender shook his head. "No, sir, she's, ah, definitely not Miss Clement."

Longarm glanced back at Millard, who shook his head. "I don't know anything about it, Parker. You'll have to go see for yourself."

"I'll do that," Longarm said. He holstered his gun and opened the door wide enough so that he could step out into the corridor. He followed the bartender back to the main room, and as they walked along the hallway, the man said, "I hated to bother you while you were talking to Mr. Millard, but the lady was very insistent that she see you."

"Well, I'm glad you fetched me then," said Longarm, deliberately keeping his tone light. "A fella never likes to keep a lady waiting for too long."

They stepped out into the main room of the club, and Longarm's companion pointed toward the bar. "There she is, over there."

Longarm looked where he was pointing and stopped short in surprise.

Standing nervously near the end of the bar, darting occasional glances at the door as if she thought this was a bad idea and wanted to flee, was Claudette.

Chapter 10

Longarm managed to overcome his surprise enough to put a smile of welcome on his face as he got his muscles working again and walked toward Claudette. He held out his hands and took hold of both of hers. "It's good to see you," he said honestly. "What are you doing here?"

"Thought I come to see you, me," she said. "Time I got away from that bayou, you bet."

The words were brave, but Longarm wasn't sure how sincere they were. There was a look in her eyes like a wild animal might have had after being dropped down in a place like this. The crowd inside the Brass Pelican, though small by some standards, probably seemed huge to her. And the noise—the piano, the spinning of the roulette wheel, the shrill laughter and coarse talk—had to be unsettling to someone accustomed to the whisper of the wind and the cry of the loon.

Some of the club's customers were openly staring at her too, which had to make her even more nervous. Longarm took her arm, clasping it just above the elbow in a gentle grip, and led her toward one of the empty tables. "Let's sit down," he suggested.

He noticed that Millard had emerged from the door to the rear corridor and was watching them curiously, but he didn't approach them. Millard had to be wondering who Claudette was, thought Longarm.

At the moment, she didn't look much like the bayou gal she had been the last time Longarm had seen her. She had cleaned herself up and was wearing a simple, inexpensive gray dress. The other women in the Brass Pelican were dressed in much finer clothes, but none of them could hold a candle to Claudette when it came to sheer beauty. Her nervousness had reminded Longarm of a wild animal; she had a wild animal's fresh, unspoiled, clean-limbed beauty as well. Which did even more than her clothes to make her seem out of place in the gambling club.

Longarm held her chair for her and then sat down beside her. "I'm mighty flattered you'd come all this way to see me," he told her. "You didn't have to do that."

"I wanted to. Been too long in the bayous, me. The world is big-big. Thought it was time to see some more of her."

Longarm could understand that. He had been fiddle-footed himself after the war, like a lot of young men. That restlessness had led him to go West, also like a lot of others. So he knew what Claudette meant about wanting to see something different. She might never be truly happy for long out of the bayou country, but for now a change of scenery wouldn't hurt her.

"How'd you find me?" he asked her. "I don't recollect mentioning that I worked here."

"You did not. I talk to that farmer man who bring you into town, I did. I know 'most ever'body round them bayous and shinneries, so it didn't take long to find him. He tell me he sees you walk off toward this street when he stop at the French Market, so I come a-knockin' on doors, askin' folks what answer if they know this mos' handsome man name of Custis."

He tried not to grin at the flattery. From what she was saying, he had made quite an impression on her. They'd had a lot of fun on the bunk in that cabin of hers, but he didn't think that was enough to bring her all the way up here.

He hoped she hadn't convinced herself that she was in love with him.

That was a sobering thought. Longarm said, "I'm glad you came for a visit, but—"

"No visit," she broke in. "Stay here in N'Awleans, I will. Get me a job." She looked around. "Maybe workin' in a place like this."

Longarm shook his head. "You don't want to work here."

"Why not? You do," she pointed out with impeccable logic.

"That's different. I'm a man, and you're—"

She pointed at one of Millard's hostesses, who was wearing a lacy, low-cut gown and hanging on the arm of a gambler at the roulette table. "I could do a job like that," said Claudette. "Look pretty an' be nice to the gentlemans."

That was true enough, Longarm supposed. Claudette was certainly pretty enough to be one of the Brass Pelican's hostesses. But he knew there was more to their job than that. Some of them worked the upstairs rooms, and they also had to make themselves available to Millard whenever he wanted one of them. Working at the Brass Pelican was a step up from whoring on the street and in the cribs—but only a step.

"Forget it," Longarm said flatly. "You don't want to work here, Claudette."

Her eyes widened with hurt. "You don't want me here, you."

"That's not it—"

"Ashamed that you even know a bayou gal like me, you bet." She started to stand up. "Well, I won't bother you no more, Custis. I be gone out of here, and you not have to see me again."

"Wait a minute, wait a minute," Longarm said in exasperation. "Let's eat this apple one bite at a time. Do you mean you're going back to the bayou country?"

She shook her head emphatically. "No. I stay here in N'Awleans, fin' me some other job to do."

Longarm sighed. If she stayed here, unaccustomed to city life, with no friends and no money, she would be working the streets within a week. He was certain of it. And he didn't want that for Claudette. She deserved better. If he got her a job here at the Brass Pelican, at least he could keep an eye on her.

"All right," he said. "I ain't promising nothing, but I'll see what I can do. I'll go talk to the boss right now."

A smile lit up her face. "You would do this for me?"

"Sure." Under his breath, he added, "Don't reckon I've got much choice."

With all the threads of the investigation he had picked up, anxious to follow them to their source, this problem with Claudette was an unwelcome distraction. But then, most of life was a distraction, and a hell of a lot of it was unwelcome, he reflected. He'd just have to make do as best he could, and by the time he wrapped up the case and left New Orleans, maybe Claudette would be ready to go back home.

While Claudette waited anxiously at the table, Longarm went over to Jasper Millard, who was standing at the end of the bar, and said, "Boss, I've got a favor to ask of you."

"I'm not sure you've been working for me long enough to ask favors, Parker," said Millard. "But then, you seem to figure you've got some special privileges."

Clearly, Millard hadn't forgotten about finding Longarm in the office. Longarm said, "I told you, that won't happen again." He shook his head. "Lord, the trouble a man gets into sometimes just because he wants a smoke."

In spite of himself, Millard chuckled. "Go ahead, Parker," he said. "Ask your favor. I'm not promising anything, but I'll listen."

"Thanks. You see that lady over there at the table, the one who came looking for me?"

Millard glanced over at Claudette, then looked again. "She's a good looker. Friend of yours?"

"You could say that. She's trying to find a job."

"And she wants to work here? She must really want to spend time around you, Parker."

Longarm gave a slight shrug. "I told her I'd ask you about it."

"Let me see . . ." Millard studied Claudette for a long moment, then said, "At first glance, she doesn't seem the type. But if she was cleaned up a little more and borrowed some dresses from the other girls . . . I suppose I could use her. *If* that's what you really want, Parker."

Longarm wasn't sure whether to be relieved or disappointed. "I'm much obliged, Boss," he told Millard. "I'll tell her she's got the job."

"Why don't you let me do that?" asked Millard, surprising Longarm. Without waiting for Longarm's reply, he sauntered over to the table where Claudette waited. Her eyes got big as he approached.

"Welcome to the Brass Pelican, my dear," Millard said as he came up to the table. He leaned over, took Claudette's hand, and brushed his lips across the back of it. It would have been difficult to say who was more surprised, Claudette or Longarm. Millard went on. "Our mutual friend Mr. Parker tells me that you'd like to work here. As it turns out, I'm in need of another hostess, so if you'd like the job . . ."

"Oh, Lordy, I sure would, me," said Claudette breathlessly. "Thank you, Mr. . . . ?"

"Millard, Jasper Millard. I'm sure we'll become very well acquainted while you're here, my dear."

Longarm's hackles rose at the suggestive tone in Millard's voice, but he drew a tight rein on his temper. Claudette was a grown woman, and she hadn't been a virgin when he met her. So she wasn't completely unaware of the ways of the world. He would look out for her as best he could, but she would also have to take care of herself. Besides, no one had appointed him her guardian.

Millard crooked a finger at one of the hostesses, a blonde

in a tight red dress. "Tessie, this is . . . I'm sorry, I don't know your name, my dear."

"Claudette," she supplied with a smile.

"This is Claudette, Tessie," continued Millard. "Take her upstairs, get her settled in, and see about arranging for the temporary loan of several gowns. Claudette's going to be working here, and since she's a friend of Mr. Parker's, I want her treated right."

The blonde glanced at Longarm, shrugged, and nodded. Clearly, the fact that Claudette was his friend didn't really mean anything to her, but she would do whatever Millard told her.

"Come on, honey," she said to Claudette. "I'll take care of you."

Claudette stood up, smiled nervously at Longarm and Millard, and followed Tessie upstairs. Millard turned to Longarm and asked, "Satisfied, Parker?"

"I reckon we'll see," said Longarm.

Tessie came back downstairs a little later and told Longarm and Millard, "This is going to take a while. I've got her soaking in a hot tub, and she doesn't act like she wants to get out. I think this might be the first real bath she's ever had!"

Longarm figured that was possible. Since it was still fairly early and the crowd in the club was still small, he said to Millard, "I think I'll go get a bite to eat, if that's all right with you, Boss?"

Millard waved a hand. "Sure, go ahead. Just don't get lost. If Annie Clement's in here tonight, I don't want her spending the whole evening asking me where you are."

Longarm grinned ruefully at the thought of Annie and Claudette being in the same place at the same time. That was a definite likelihood. He might be wise to keep them apart as much as possible.

As if reading Longarm's mind, Millard chuckled and said,

"Didn't think of that when you asked me to hire her, did you?"

"Well, to be honest, no," admitted Longarm. "But I reckon I'll just have to make the best of it now. I'll worry about it after supper."

He left the club, but he wasn't looking for something to eat. Instead, he headed for the docks. That notebook he had discovered in Millard's desk earlier in the day still bothered him. Or rather, not the notebook itself, but the information he had found written down in it. He was still intensely curious about those ships that had left New Orleans bound for Saint Laurent.

Gallatin Street was only a block away from the river, but the levee area was around the great curve of the Mississippi that gave New Orleans its nickname of the Crescent City. Where Canal Street met the waterfront was the hub of the shipping industry. Longarm spent the next hour roaming through the area. Ships were docked two and three deep at the wharves. Loading and unloading began before dawn and went on by torchlight until well after midnight. From the north came the riverboats with their tall smokestacks and their paddle wheels. The goods they brought downriver were transferred onto tall-masted sailing ships that would ply the waters of the Gulf and then head across the Atlantic to Europe. Likewise, the cargoes they brought on their return voyages were loaded onto the steamships and carried back up the mighty Mississippi. It was a thriving trade, with merchandise of every conceivable kind passing through this port.

At the moment, however, Longarm was interested only in the ships that had sailed for Saint Laurent, so he asked around until someone pointed him toward a burly black stevedore who reminded him somewhat uncomfortably of the man Longarm had been forced to kill the night before.

"Howdy," Longarm said to the man, who was taking a break after loading some crates onto a riverboat.

Immediately, the man looked suspiciously at him and said,

"What you want, Boss?" He had the lilting accent of the West Indies in his voice.

Longarm shook his head. "I ain't nobody's boss. I'm just looking for a little information."

"I don' know nothin' 'bout nothin'," the dockworker said flatly.

"I'm told you were around a few days ago when some ships left here bound for an island called Saint Laurent. The ships were the *Erasmus,* the *Bonneville*—"

"I know de ships you talkin' 'bout. Dey belong to Mr. Millard. I done worked on dem before."

Longarm was surprised the man admitted so easily that the ships belonged to Millard. He asked, "Did you load them this time?"

"No, Boss," the man said with a fervent shake of his head. "Mr. Millard's men, dey load dem ships, tell us to stay away from 'em."

Longarm frowned. "So there was cargo on the ships when they sailed, but none of the regular dockworkers loaded it?"

"No, Boss. Dey load dem ships in de middle o' de night, so nobody aroun'. Why you wanna know 'bout dis? You a lawman?"

That guess hit way too close to home. Longarm laughed harshly, then declared, "Not hardly. I'm just a fella who's got an interest in what Millard does."

The dockworker stood up quickly and began to move away. "You jus' leave me outta dis, Boss," he said, sounding frightened now. "Don' wan' nothin' t' do with dat Royale. You white folks jus' keeps your troubles to yourselves."

"Wait a minute—"

But the man wouldn't listen to Longarm. He hurried away, casting nervous glances over his shoulder as he did so.

Well, at least he had learned a few things, Longarm told himself. The ships had definitely been carrying cargo when they left New Orleans bound for Saint Laurent, but that cargo was a secret and had been taken on board under cover of night by Millard's own men, rather than the usual dock-workers.

Word of the intensifying conflict between Millard and Royale had reached the docks too. In fact, the man Longarm had just been talking to had taken him for an agent of Royale's. Longarm hoped that suspicion didn't get back to Millard's ears any time soon. Millard already seemed to trust him a little less after the incident in the office.

Longarm stopped and got a quick bite to eat on his way back to the gambling club. The streets were growing busier. In fact, the crowds were building to a downright throng. With a frown, Longarm stopped and thought about what day it was, then closed his eyes and winced.

It was Fat Tuesday. Mardi Gras. Tonight would be the busiest night of the year in New Orleans, complete with the traditional parade with showy, elaborate floats put together by the krewes, the societies devoted to such activities. The celebration would go on until dawn, at least. What a night for Claudette to start working at the Brass Pelican.

Longarm shook his head and moved on, grinning at the costumed people who were beginning to appear on the streets. He saw men masquerading as devils, pirates, wild Indians, and clowns. Women seemed to prefer more sedate costumes. Many of them were made up to look like Marie Antoinette, complete with beauty spots, powdered wigs, and gowns cut so low that often the upper rings of their nipples were visible. It was already a spectacle, and would be more so before the night was over.

When he reached the club, practically the first thing he saw was Claudette. She was wearing a blue gown that went well with her hair and eyes, and glittery earrings dangled from her ears. Her hair was piled atop her head in an elaborate arrangement of curls that made her look much more sophisticated than the simple bayou girl he had met a couple of days earlier. It was a little difficult to believe that she was the same person.

But as she saw him and came hurrying toward him, smiling broadly, he had no trouble recognizing her. She practically threw herself into his arms and hugged him.

"Oh, Custis, these clothes, she is so nice I never dream I wear such a thing, me," she exclaimed. "Thank you, thank you so much."

"You're welcome," Longarm told her. "If this is what you really want, Claudette, then I'm glad I could help you get it. You sure gave me a hand." He lowered his voice. "Speaking of that, you didn't say anything to Mr. Millard about how you helped me get away from those old boys the other day, did you?"

She shook her head, her smile disappearing to be replaced by a solemn expression. "This I did not do yet, Custis. You don't want Mr. Millard to know about it?"

"I'd just as soon we kept it between us. Not because I ain't grateful to you or anything, because I am, but—"

She shook her head and put a fingertip on his lips. "Don't say any more, you. You got your reasons, and I don't need to know 'em."

"That's mighty understanding of you."

She came up on her tiptoes, and instead of her finger, she brushed his lips with hers. "I do just about anything for you, Custis, no questions, no explanation. I guarantee."

Longarm slipped an arm around her waist and pulled her closer to him, giving her a proper kiss. Claudette's body melded against his. This was a mighty public place for such an embrace, thought Longarm, but he didn't rightly care. Besides, a man and a woman hugging and kissing was probably downright normal compared to some of the things that went on here from time to time, he speculated. Nobody seemed to be paying any attention to them.

Then he heard the voice right behind him saying, "Well, well, what have we here?" He froze as he realized it belonged to Paul Clement.

And wherever Paul was, Longarm thought as he stifled a groan, Annie was usually right with him.

Chapter 11

For a second, Longarm was afraid to turn around. He expected to hear Annie's voice lashing at him, demanding to know who in the hell Claudette was and just why she was in his arms with his lips pressed to hers.

But when Annie's voice didn't come, Longarm glanced over his shoulder and saw that Clement was standing there alone, the smile on his face even more mocking than usual. He walked slowly around them, and his gaze was frankly admiring as he looked at Claudette. "Hello," he said. "I don't believe we've met."

"This is Claudette," said Longarm. "She's a good friend of mine."

"Yes," Clement said dryly, "I could tell."

"Claudette, this is Monsieur Paul Clement."

Clement took Claudette's hand, bent over it, and kissed it as Millard had done. Claudette said, "Honored to meet you, M'sieu Clement, I surely am." She was almost glowing from all the masculine attention that was being paid to her today, and as he looked at the radiant expression on her face, Longarm thought that maybe getting her a job here hadn't been such a bad idea after all.

Cautiously, Longarm asked Clement, "Where's your sister?"

"Annie will be along shortly. She wanted her costume for tonight to be perfect."

"Costume?" repeated Longarm. Clement was wearing his normal evening clothes.

"Yes, this is Mardi Gras, remember?" Clement reached into his pocket, brought out a piece of black silk, and unfolded it to reveal that it was a mask. He placed it over his eyes and tied the strings attached to it behind his head. "The whole thing is a bit silly, I know, but one can't argue with tradition, can one?"

"I've heard of Mardi Gras," said Claudette, "but I didn't know it was tonight."

"Well, then, you're in for a treat, *mademoiselle,*" Clement said as he moved smoothly alongside Claudette and slipped his arm through hers. "If you'll be so kind as to keep me company while I'm trying my luck at the blackjack table, I'll tell you all about it."

Claudette glanced at Longarm, and he gave a barely perceptible nod to let her know that it was all right with him for her to go with Clement. He didn't have any hold over her, and the sooner she understood that, the better, especially if she wanted to work here at the Brass Pelican.

As Clement and Claudette moved off toward the blackjack table, Clement tossed a look over his shoulder at Longarm, who nodded to him in gratitude. Annie would be here soon, thought Longarm, and it would be better all around if Claudette was distracted. Clement had proven surprisingly understanding about the matter.

Sure enough, not ten more minutes had gone by when Annie appeared, pausing just inside the doorway of the club to look around for Longarm. He happened to be looking in that direction when she came in, and although he didn't recognize her at first, as soon as his eyes met hers he knew her.

She was wearing a gypsy costume, with an embroidered white blouse that left both shoulders bare and a neckline that

111

plunged low enough to reveal practically all of the creamy valley between her breasts. A bright red skirt, also decorated with embroidery, swirled around her ankles. Golden hoop earrings and a wig with curls as black as midnight completed the costume. She was wearing a mask too, like her brother.

Her face assumed a coy expression as Longarm approached her. "Would you like to have your fortune told?" she asked over the music and laughter that filled the room. Even raised so that he could hear, her voice seemed to contain a purr.

Longarm extended his hand toward her. "Sure. Just don't tell me I'm going to meet a beautiful woman, 'cause I already have."

She took his right hand in her left, then used the index finger of her right hand to trace the lines on his palm. Her long, red-painted nail dug almost painfully into his skin. "You will meet many beautiful women, but only one is right for you. If you ignore her, you will be in much danger."

Longarm chuckled. "I reckon I'd better pay a lot of attention to her then." He reached up and cupped her chin, tilting her head back so that he could bring his mouth down on hers.

He sure hoped Paul Clement was keeping Claudette occupied.

For the second time in less than a half hour, he was kissing a beautiful woman and molding the soft warmth of her body against his as he drew her into an embrace. A different woman, at that. All the hazards of his life as a federal lawman didn't quite measure up to that, he thought wryly. He was really living dangerously now.

"Come on," he said to Annie as he broke the kiss. "I'll buy you a drink."

Annie nodded. "But not too many drinks tonight," she said. "I want you to take me home tonight, Custis."

"If I can," promised Longarm. How the night ended up, though, really depended on Millard, and Royale, and even Claudette.

Longarm stayed close by Annie as the long evening began to roll by. The club was too crowded and noisy to do much more than sit at a table, try to carry on a conversation in half-shouts, and hope that they didn't get trampled by the mob. Worry gnawed at the back of Longarm's brain. As packed in as the customers were tonight, anything that went wrong could easily turn into a catastrophe. It was a perfect opportunity for Royale to strike again at Millard.

But despite the crowd and the noise, the night's festivities went fairly peacefully. A few men got a little boisterous from too much to drink, but Millard's bouncers handled them with ease. Millard came over to the table while Annie had gone to use the facilities, which were indoors rather than out back of the building, a luxury Longarm hadn't expected to find in a place like the Brass Pelican. With a nod to Longarm, Millard sat down and said, "I was halfway expecting trouble tonight."

"You and me both, Boss," Longarm told him. "I reckon Royale must be celebrating Mardi Gras like everybody else."

"Let's hope so."

Claudette swept over to the table then, followed by Paul Clement. She was laughing brightly at something Clement had said. "Custis!" she greeted Longarm, and from the level of her merriment, he figured she had been sipping on a few drinks this evening. "Paul, he is going to take me to watch the Mardi Gras parade. Why don't you and his sister come with us?"

Longarm swallowed hard. "Sister?" he repeated.

"Oh, don't worry, Custis," said Clement. "I told Claudette how kind you've been to my poor maiden sister, paying attention to her while we're here in New Orleans."

Longarm took back what he had thought earlier about Clement being understanding. He was a damn rabble-rouser! But there was nothing Longarm could do now except plunge ahead and be thankful that Claudette seemed to be in a good mood.

"Sure," Longarm said. "I don't reckon I've ever seen a

Mardi Gras parade, so I wouldn't mind at all." He looked at Millard. "If it's all right with you, Boss."

"Go ahead," Millard said with a wave of his hand. "Like you said, Royale's probably celebrating tonight too. He might even be at the parade. Who knows?"

Claudette looked at Longarm. "Who is this Royale, Custis? Another of your ladyfriends, maybe?"

"Not hardly," Longarm replied vehemently. "Just a . . . business associate, I suppose you could say. Nothing for you to worry about."

Clement looked across the room and said, "Here comes Annie now."

It took a few minutes for Annie to make her way through the crowd. Even in the press of people, Longarm had no trouble spotting her in that colorful outfit. As she came up to the table, he stood and reached out to take her hand. "We're going out to watch the Mardi Gras parade, if that's all right with you," he said.

"Of course. I'd like that." Annie looked at Claudette and went on. "I don't believe we've met."

Clement began, "She's a friend of—"

"A friend of your brother, me," Claudette cut in. She put out her hand and shook with Annie. "Claudette, that is my name."

"What a pretty name," said Annie. "And that gown and those earrings are beautiful. You and Paul are coming to the parade too, aren't you?"

"Of course. I would not miss my first Mardi Gras parade."

Longarm tried not to heave a sigh of relief. Claudette was really helping him out. Most women would have been spitting jealous, but she was going out of her way to keep the peace with Annie for tonight. He would have to thank her later if he got the chance. And he hoped that Paul Clement's big grin didn't tip off Annie that something more was going on than was readily apparent.

With Annie on his arm and Claudette being accompanied

by Clement, Longarm shouldered his way through the crowd and led the little group to the door. As they stepped out onto Gallatin Street, the press of people around them lessened slightly, but the sidewalks and the cobblestone street itself were still unusually crowded. All the street lamps had been lit, and light flooded out through open doors and windows so that the revelers could see what they were doing. Everywhere, purple and green and gold—the official colors of Mardi Gras—were dominant, and hundreds, perhaps even thousands, of voices were singing the anthem of Mardi Gras, "If Ever I Cease to Love." Longarm found himself humming along with the tune as he and his companions made their way through the throng.

"Come on," Annie cried merrily as she tugged on Longarm's hand. "The parade is on St. Charles Avenue."

That seemed to be the direction the crowd was flowing, all right, thought Longarm. He was glad he wasn't trying to go the other way. It would be like trying to swim upstream against a strong current.

Claudette and Paul Clement were still talking animatedly. Longarm knew it was unreasonable, considering the way he had felt earlier, but now he was the one who was a mite jealous. Obviously, Claudette had been telling the truth: It wasn't so much seeing him again that had brought her to New Orleans. It was an honest desire to try something new in her life—an attempt to leave the bayous behind her. Longarm wished her the best of luck in the effort.

Longarm hadn't been to the hotel much in the past few days, but he had been aware of the sound of hammering whenever he went in and out of the place. Now he understood the reason why. Viewing stands had been built all along the avenue, and they were already packed. It was doubtful that Longarm and the others would be able to find a place to sit. They would have to stand along the sidewalks with the hundreds of others who had gotten there a little too late to fit into the viewing stands.

Annie noticed the same thing and mentioned it, then said,

"But that's all right. When the floats pass by, we'll be able to catch some of the things the crew members toss down as they pass by."

She went on to explain the tradition to Longarm and Claudette. Each year, the members of the societies that built the floats threw candy, flowers, and coins to the spectators who lined the parade route. The gifts were meant primarily for the children . . . but at Mardi Gras, everyone was a child, at least to a certain extent.

Longarm, Annie, Claudette, and Paul Clement managed to find a place to stand near the front of the crowd. They were just in time, because not far away, someone shouted, "Here they come!"

Annie leaned closer to Longarm's ear and called over the clamor, "Rex, the King of Mardi Gras, will be on the last float! It's quite an honor for the gentleman selected."

Longarm supposed that was the case. He would have felt mighty funny dressing up in a mask and a gold crown and a long, fur-lined cape, so he was just as glad that he would never be the King of Mardi Gras.

The huge, elaborate floats began rolling by, pushed along on their wheeled platforms by krewe members who were concealed under the layers of flowers and bunting. Cheers went up from the crowd as the costumed men atop the floats began tossing their gifts over the heads of the spectators. It seemed to be raining candy and flowers and coins. Longarm grinned and ducked his head as a particularly heavy shower of gifts pelted him. Beside him, Annie was gleefully plucking items out of the air. On the other side of her, Claudette was doing the same thing. Children swarmed around them, darting between them to scoop up the treats that had fallen to the sidewalk.

Someone bumped heavily into Longarm from behind, and taken by surprise, he stumbled forward a step. As he caught his balance, he glanced back to see who had run into him, forcing down the irritation that was welling up inside him.

Mardi Gras was no time to be losing his temper just because some old son was clumsy.

The light from a torch on one of the passing floats glinted off steel. Longarm's eyes widened as he saw a man in a pirate costume thrusting a short cutlass at him.

He would feel foolish if the cutlass turned out to be rubber and the "pirate" only playing, but Longarm had learned a long time ago it was better to be foolish than dead. He twisted, letting the blade pass harmlessly by him, and clamped his left arm down on the arm of the man holding the weapon. He drove his right fist into the man's midsection, sinking it almost to the wrist. Breath puffed out of the man's mouth.

Longarm caught hold of his wrist and wrenched it, forcing the pirate to drop the blade. It clattered to the cobblestones, and the sound told Longarm that the cutlass was most definitely the real thing. For some reason, this piratical reveler had just tried to kill him.

Close by, a woman screamed.

Longarm brought his fist up and slammed it into the pirate's jaw. The blow didn't travel more than half a foot, but it had all of Longarm's strength behind it. The would-be killer's head slewed to the side, and he sagged against Longarm, stunned. Longarm let go of him and stepped back, allowing the man to slide to the ground. He didn't want the pirate to be trampled to death, but that scream had sounded like Annie, and he was more interested in making sure she was all right. He looked urgently through the crowd for her.

She was gone.

So was her brother, Longarm saw. No sign of Paul Clement met his searching gaze. Of course, in this crowd someone could be only a few feet away and be invisible. Claudette was still there, looking surprised and more than a little frightened. Longarm leaned close to her and shouted, "What happened?"

"Paul and Annie, they are gone, them!" she replied. "I did not see where they went—"

Longarm wasn't surprised. No one in the wildly celebrating crowd had even noticed when the pirate tried to run him through. Everyone was too caught up in the excitement of Mardi Gras.

Which meant it was a damn good time to get rid of some enemies without anyone noticing.

"Royale," muttered Longarm through clenched teeth.

"What did you say?" asked Claudette, looking worried.

Longarm shook his head. "Nothing. Let's get you out of here, and then I'll find Paul and Annie."

He hoped he could make good on that statement. Royale clearly had spies everywhere, and he would know that the Clements were regular customers and friends of Jasper Millard's. It seemed unlikely that Royale would try to strike at Millard by hurting Annie and Paul . . . but none of Royale's other recent attempts had worked out exactly as planned. Royale could be getting desperate enough to kidnap the Clements and use them to try to force some concessions from Millard.

Those thoughts raced through Longarm's brain in an instant as he gripped Claudette's arm and attempted to wedge a path through the crowd for them. Everyone was pushing forward, trying to get closer to the floats that were still passing by, and once again Longarm was struck by the similarity to swimming upstream. He and Claudette were making only scanty progress.

How he heard the gun being cocked over the uproar was beyond him. Maybe it was instinct again. But something made him jerk around in time to see the little pistol being pointed at him by an Indian—or somebody made up to look like an Indian. Longarm's hand shot out and grabbed the barrel of the gun, twisting it upward just as it cracked spitefully. He heard the wicked whine of the bullet passing close beside his ear. It struck his hat and sent it spinning off his head. The Indian tried to bring the gun back to bear, but Longarm held it off while he brought his other hand up in a jabbing blow. With people all around him, there was no room to swing the roundhouse punch he wanted to throw.

The jab was good enough. The Indian's head rocked back, and the pistol slipped from his fingers. Longarm shoved him away and turned back to Claudette, hoping nothing had happened to her.

She was still there, but the crowd around her was clearing out a little. The gunshot had been loud enough to carry to the ears of the nearest revelers, and they were scurrying for cover. Several men shouted angry questions, and a couple of women cried out in fear. Longarm just grabbed Claudette's arm again and took advantage of the opportunity to plunge through the momentary opening in the crowd.

The whole place might be full of assassins, he realized. Like a damn fool, he had come out here to have a good time, and Royale's hired killers had followed him. He still had no idea what had happened to Annie and Paul, but there was no time to search for them now. He had to get Claudette to someplace where she would be safe.

For several yards, they were able to hurry along the sidewalk, but then the crowd closed in around them again. These people further along the block had not heard the shot, and did not know that a murder attempt was occurring in their midst. Frustrated, Longarm tightened his grip on Claudette's hand and pulled her toward the only open space he saw.

Together, they ran into the street, darting between two of the floats.

A startled shout went up from the krewe members on the next float in line. Longarm turned and began running alongside the colorful procession, tugging Claudette along with him. It was as if they were part of the parade, despite the fact that neither of them wore costumes. More shouts of surprise trailed them. Interfering with the Mardi Gras parade was unheard of. Not even those who had drunk far too much champagne would dare such a thing.

Longarm looked back and saw that he and Claudette weren't the only ones ignoring tradition tonight. Several men were pursuing them: a clown, a devil, and a man in the buckskins and coonskin cap of an early-day frontiersman. Dan Rice, Satan, and Davy Crockett, Longarm thought wildly. But the guns in their hands made them a deadly trio.

Those guns began to bang, and again there were screams as the crowd broke and ran for cover. The parade came to a screeching halt. Longarm ducked around another float, crossing back to the side of the street where he and Claudette had started. The would-be killers veered after them, firing again. Longarm heard bullets whip past his head, and hoped that the stray shots didn't hit anybody in the crowd.

He hoped as well that Captain Denton had some officers assigned to the parade route, but so far Longarm hadn't seen any police. Maybe they knew better than to interfere with Mardi Gras. It was certainly beginning to look like Longarm couldn't count on any help from that quarter.

Shoving Claudette on ahead of him, he turned and palmed out his Colt. He took careful aim and squeezed off a quick shot, and the clown stumbled, clutching at the leg Longarm's bullet had just ventilated. The brightly garbed killer tumbled off his feet, shouting curses. The Devil and Davy Crockett came on without slowing down. The guns in their hands blasted.

Longarm turned and ran again, thankful that Claudette hadn't slowed while he paused to cut down the odds. She was several yards in front of him now. She threw a frightened glance over her shoulder to make sure he was still behind her.

The mouth of an alley loomed up on their right. "In there!" called Longarm, indicating the alley with a wave of his gun hand as Claudette looked back again. She made the turn, stumbling only a little as she did so. Longarm plunged into the gloom of the alley behind her. Here in the thick shadows, Claudette was forced to slow down, and he caught up with her in a matter of seconds.

"Custis—!" she panted, breathless from both exertion and fear.

"Keep going," he told her. "I'll slow them down again."

As he stopped and turned, he saw two figures loom up at the mouth of the alley, silhouetted by the light from the street behind them. One shape was indistinct, but the other was clearly marked by horns and a tail. Longarm triggered twice, aiming low. The muzzle blasts lit up the alley for an instant like orange lightning, and the roar of the shots was deafening in these narrow confines. Longarm couldn't tell if he had done any damage or not. Both of the pursuers fired, and brick chips thrown out by the bullets as they struck the building beside Longarm stung his face.

Behind him somewhere, Claudette let out a scream and shouted, "Custis!" Her voice was filled with mortal fear.

Longarm whirled around, leery of turning his back to the assassins, but knowing that he had to see what was happening to Claudette. He ran down the alley, heedless of any obstacles that might be in his path, veering from side to side to make himself a more difficult target. Suddenly, without any warning, he emerged into a small rear courtyard behind the buildings, and enough light came from the windows for him to see what was going on.

Despite the warmth of the night, his blood froze at the scene laid out before him.

Claudette was struggling in the grip of a huge black man in work clothes. She flailed at him and clawed his face, but he didn't seem to even feel the blows. He wasn't trying to hurt her, but he was holding her in an unbreakable grip.

Another man was shuffling toward Longarm, arms outstretched, his face as dull and lacking in expression as that of his companion. Longarm took one look at him and uttered a heartfelt, "Shit!"

The Devil and Davy Crockett behind him, bent on filling him full of lead, and a pair of equally murderous zombies in front of him . . .

It was times like this that made a fella wonder why he had ever pinned on a lawman's badge in the first place.

Chapter 12

The two pursuers burst out of the alley into the courtyard and opened fire just as the dead-eyed man lunged toward Longarm. Longarm threw himself to the side, rolling out of the way. The gunmen couldn't stop their trigger fingers in time, and several shots roared out.

But instead of hitting Longarm, the bullets thudded into the broad chest of the huge black man who had tried to grab him. Just as before, the slugs barely slowed the man. Unable to stop his single-minded charge, he crashed into the two costumed bushwhackers. They yelled in horror as his hands found their throats. More shots roared, the explosions muffled by the huge body.

Longarm came up in a crouch, knowing that for the time being at least, three of his enemies were occupied with each other. That left Claudette, who was still struggling in the grip of the other . . . well, zombie. There was nothing else to call them, thought Longarm. He reversed his hold on the Colt and threw himself at the figures swaying in the shadows.

Even in this gloom, he could make out the man who towered over Claudette. Longarm brought the Colt down, slamming the butt of the gun against the back of the man's skull. There was no response, so he struck again and then again. Finally, after the third blow, the man shoved Claudette aside and swung around toward Longarm, his movements slow and lumbering but no less dangerous.

From the corner of his eye, Longarm saw Claudette stumble backwards to lean against the side of a building as she gasped for breath. He flipped the gun around so that its barrel pointed toward the huge shape. Even though he knew he was probably wasting his breath, he said harshly, "Hold it right there, old son! I don't want to have to kill you!"

These men, entranced just like the first one who had stalked Longarm, were not acting of their own accord. Longarm was convinced of that. Someone had put a spell on them—or drugged them, that was the more rational explanation—and sent them after him. Who had done that, and why, he didn't know. Royale was the best bet, but he had no proof that Royale used voodoo. The zombies looked like dockworkers. They were probably innocent men who had been turned into living weapons, and now that he knew what he was facing, Longarm didn't want to have to shoot them.

But there might not be any other way to stop them. Even now, the second man, the one who had been hit by several shots from the two gunmen, was climbing ponderously back to his feet, leaving two motionless figures sprawled on the alley floor behind him, their heads set at odd angles. The Devil and Davy Crockett had come to a bad end.

And so would Longarm and Claudette if they didn't get out of here.

One advantage they had over the creatures was that the zombies were slow. Longarm darted around the one coming toward him, easily avoiding a clumsy swipe of the man's hamlike hand. He grabbed Claudette's arm and said, "Come on!"

They broke into a run, dashing from the courtyard into another alley that opened off it. Once again Longarm and

Claudette raced along blindly, convinced that anything they might run into in the darkness wouldn't be as bad as what was behind them. For a moment, Longarm could hear the shuffling sounds of pursuit, but then the noises faded away as he and Claudette emerged onto another street. He had no idea where they were. They were among people again, though, and he was grateful for that. This street was nowhere near as packed as St. Charles Avenue had been, but there were enough revelers on the sidewalks for them to be able to blend into the crowd. Longarm slid his gun back into its holster before anyone could notice it, then led Claudette in a fast walk along the sidewalk. They weaved in and out of the celebrating pedestrians.

Quite a few people on this street were wearing costumes too, but none of them paid any attention to Longarm and Claudette. Longarm hoped that the pirate, the Indian, the clown, the devil, and the frontiersman had been the only assassins after him tonight. But who had sent them, and why had those zombies popped up like that? Had *they* been trailing him too? And what the hell had happened to Paul and Annie Clement? Longarm figured he had better get back to the Brass Pelican and find out if Millard had heard anything. If Royale had kidnapped the Clements, it had to be because of their connection with Millard, so it was natural to assume that he would get in touch with Millard to present his ransom demands.

Longarm's jaw tightened. He hoped like blazes that the next time around, Billy Vail would assign him to a case that was a mite simpler—like finding one particular blade of grass in the whole damned Great Plains!

After a few minutes, Longarm got his bearings and turned toward the waterfront. Claudette's hand tightened on his arm. "Custis," she said, "what are we to do?"

"I have to find out if Millard knows anything about what happened to Annie and Paul," said Longarm. "It's a pretty complicated business, Claudette, but Millard has an enemy who might try to get at him through his friends."

Claudette nodded. "This enemy, he is a voodoo priest, no?"

"Now, I just don't know about that," Longarm answered honestly.

"Only a priest or priestess of *voudun* could send those zombies after you."

Longarm shot a glance at her. "You know about things like that?"

"Gran'pere, his gran'mama was from Haiti. The slavers, they bring her there from Africa, long, long ago. *Voudun* was a religion there, and she was a high priestess, you see. She know all them rituals and how the religion got turned into voodoo . . . black magic. As a boy, Gran'pere hear the stories she tell, and he believe, you bet. I remember once, he been feudin' with this other fella who live round the bayou, and Gran'pere come to N'Awleans, buy himself a *gris-gris*—what you call a black magic charm—from Marie Laveau. He leave it on the fella's doorstep, and that fella, he get sick and like to die."

"But he didn't die?" asked Longarm, interested in this bizarre tale.

Claudette shook her head. "No. But he would have, you bet, if he had not come up here and bought a *gris-gris* of his own from the Voodoo Queen, what they call Marie Laveau."

"So he bought something to ward off the black magic your granddaddy sicced on him."

Claudette nodded.

"And he bought it from the same person who sold the original charm to Gran'pere," said Longarm.

"That is right."

Despite the harrowing night he had had, Longarm had to chuckle. "So this Marie Laveau gets 'em coming and going. Sounds like a pretty smart businesswoman."

Claudette stared at him, aghast at his lack of respect. "She is the Voodoo Queen!"

"Then maybe she's the lady I need to talk to if I want to find out who's been sending those zombies after me."

Claudette's eyes widened. "You have seen the zombies before tonight?"

"One of 'em tried to wring my neck a few nights ago," Longarm told her.

She shuddered and said, "You are a lucky man, you. Zombies come after a man, he wind up dead most all the time."

"I don't intend to let any zombie drag me back into the grave with him," declared Longarm. "I hate to ask it, but since you know something about this stuff, would you be willing to help me find this Marie Laveau?"

Again, Claudette shuddered. "It is not hard to find her. She lives in a little house on St. Anne Street. A fella who was grateful to her because she help his son give her the house. It belong to her for the rest of her days."

"You know where it is?"

She nodded. "I know."

"Will you show me?"

Stubbornly, Claudette shook her head. "I will not do this thing."

"But—"

She interrupted his protest. "I will go there and speak to Marie Laveau for you, Custis. I be safe there, but maybe you wouldn't be, no. Better for me to go by myself first."

"Damn it, that's not what I want. I don't want anything to happen to you."

She stopped and smiled up at him. Down the block, several men were serenading some women who leaned over the wrought-iron railing of a balcony on the second floor of one of the buildings. As the drunken, out-of-tune strains of "If Ever I Cease to Love" filled the night, Claudette put her hand on the back of Longarm's neck and pulled his head down to hers. Her mouth found his.

"I do this for you, Custis," she whispered as she broke the kiss. "Don't worry, you. The Voodoo Queen got no reason to put a spell on me."

"Well, all right," Longarm said grudgingly. "But be mighty careful."

"I will come to your hotel when I find out anything."

Longarm nodded and told her the room number. "Aren't you coming back to the Brass Pelican now?"

She shook her head. "No. Tell Mr. Millard how very sorry I am, but I have a more important job now, you bet. I help you find out who are your enemies, no?"

She had unofficially deputized herself, thought Longarm, and he had allowed such a thing to happen. When this case was over, he might have to be a little creative in the report he wrote for Billy Vail.

But then, a lot of things had already happened that Billy wasn't likely to believe!

Longarm kissed her again and repeated, "Be careful."

With a smile and a wave, Claudette left him there, a few blocks from Gallatin Street. He sighed as he watched her disappear into the crowd. There were still plenty of revelers abroad on this night of nights. Longarm turned and made his way through them, heading for the Brass Pelican. He still had to find out if Millard had heard anything about Paul and Annie Clement.

"What the hell happened to you?"

Millard greeted him with that growled question as Longarm came up to the bar in the Brass Pelican a few minutes later. Before Longarm could answer, Millard went on. "Paul Clement said you got in some kind of a fight at the Mardi Gras parade."

"Clement's been here?" asked Longarm sharply.

"Of course. He and his sister came back here earlier. They said you and that girl Claudette ran off together, that there was a fight and some shooting."

"Paul and Annie were all right?"

Millard frowned. "They were shaken up a little, but yeah, they were all right. What's going on here, Parker? You're acting mighty strange."

Longarm felt a surge of relief. So Annie and Clement had just gotten separated from him in the crowd and hadn't been

127

kidnapped by Royale after all. He looked around the room. "Are they here now?"

Millard shook his head. "No, they left a little while ago. Annie was upset by everything that had happened. She was worried about you, Parker. Now, damn it, I want some answers."

"Royale," said Longarm. "He had some men dressed up in Mardi Gras costumes, and they followed us through the crowd and tried to kill me at the parade."

"Son of a bitch!" Millard's hands curled into fists. "Every time I start to hope maybe that bastard's given up, he tries something else. Were you hurt? What about Claudette?"

"We got away from Royale's men after I winged one of 'em." That was almost the truth, thought Longarm. He was just leaving out any mention of zombies. No need to spook Millard—or make the man think he was crazy. "I don't know if Claudette's coming back here to the club or not. She was pretty shaken up by the whole thing too. She's spent most of her life in the bayou country. She may have decided she doesn't much like New Orleans after all."

"Blast it!" exclaimed Millard. "She was a mighty pretty little thing. I was looking forward to getting to know her better."

I'll just bet you were, old son, thought Longarm. He knew exactly how Millard intended to get to know Claudette better. Maybe she was safer going to see that so-called Voodoo Queen after all.

"At least everything's been peaceful here," continued Millard. He swept a hand around to indicate the crowd of gamblers and drinkers, many of them attired in costumes. "This is going to be one of the most profitable nights of the year."

"*If* Royale doesn't butt in again," Longarm pointed out.

Millard glowered and nodded in agreement.

Longarm spent the rest of the night in the Brass Pelican, and as Millard had predicted, it was a lucrative evening for the club. The place was still doing a booming business as the new day dawned.

"Go home," Millard said to a yawning Longarm. "We've made it through the night, and I don't think Royale's going to try anything now."

Longarm nodded. He was anxious to return to the St. Charles and see if Claudette had shown up there following her visit to Marie Laveau. Bareheaded, since he hadn't had a chance to retrieve the planter's hat that had been shot off in the ambush attempt, he left the club and walked through streets littered almost ankle-deep with the debris of the previous night's celebration. Quite a few people were still on the sidewalks, most of them staggering along drunkenly in costumes disheveled by hours of partying. In the light of dawn, everything that had seemed so colorful and exotic the night before now appeared faintly seedy and disreputable.

Longarm stopped at the desk of the St. Charles and asked the sleepy-eyed clerk on duty, "Has a young woman been here looking for me?"

The man shook his head. "No, sir, not that I recall. Let me check your box for messages." He looked around, then shook his head again. "Afraid not, sir."

Longarm felt a sharp pang of disappointment and worry. He had thought that Claudette might be waiting for him in the lobby or even up in his room, if she had been able to persuade the clerk or one of the bellmen to let her in. He said, "If a lady—young, attractive, dark hair, talks with a Cajun accent—shows up, send her right up to my room, will you?"

Even as sleepy as he was, the clerk managed to smirk a little as he gave Longarm his room key. "Of course, Mr. Parker. Right away."

Longarm ignored the man's knowing grin and headed for the stairs. He was too tired and concerned about Claudette to care about anything else.

He had thrust the key into the lock and was about to turn it when he froze suddenly. Out of habit, he had glanced down

129

before opening the door, and he saw that the end of the match he had closed between the door and the jamb when he left the room the night before was now gone. It was an old trick, one that he used frequently when he was staying in a strange place, and it had saved his life more than once. He always put the match just an inch or two above the floor, so that anybody opening the door wouldn't notice it when it fell.

But he noticed when it was gone, as it was now, and its absence warned him that somebody had been in his room while he was gone. Might even still be there, he thought.

He had paused only an instant in opening the door, such a short time that his hesitation had probably gone unnoticed by anyone lurking inside. He twisted the key the rest of the way as he drew his gun, then in one smooth movement he drove his shoulder into the door so that it slammed open as he went into the room in a rolling dive. He came up in a crouch, the Colt held tightly in his hand, ready to fire.

Claudette sat up sharply in bed, gasping in surprise and holding the sheet in front of her bare breasts.

"Custis!" she exclaimed. "What—"

Longarm came to his feet and kicked the door shut. "Are you alone?" he asked.

Claudette let the sheet drop, revealing the firm globes of her breasts. She patted the pillow next to her. "Do you see anyone else in here?" she asked.

Longarm had to admit that he didn't. She was undoubtedly by herself in the bed—a situation he intended to remedy as soon as possible. Just looking at her pebbled nipples made some of his weariness go away.

He holstered his gun. "Sorry about busting in here like that," he said. "I didn't think you were here. I asked about you down in the lobby, and the clerk said no one had shown up looking for me."

"I came in the back way and persuaded one of the bellmen to let me into your room," she explained. "No one in the lobby saw me."

Longarm didn't ask how she had convinced the bellman

to cooperate with her. Probably the less he knew about that, the better. He shucked his gunbelt and coat and vest, then began taking off his shirt and tie. "Did you find Marie Laveau?" he asked.

"I saw her. I spoke to her, me." Claudette sounded as if she found that difficult to believe even now. "But she would tell me nothing, Custis. She remember my gran'pere, though, and his gran'mama before him."

Longarm frowned as he sat down in a chair and pulled off his boots. "Just how old *is* this Voodoo Queen anyway?"

"No one knows," said Claudette with a shake of her head. "She is old, very old."

"Did she send those zombies after me?"

"She would not admit it if she did, her. But I think maybe so."

Longarm sighed. "Looks like I'm going to have to go see her myself, maybe buy myself a magic charm to ward off walking dead men."

And if he did, he couldn't wait to see Billy Vail's face when he put in an expense voucher for it!

Claudette threw the sheet aside, revealing her body in all its glorious nudity. "Come to me, Custis, and hold me, you. I want to forget all about voodoo and zombies and men with guns for a while."

Longarm certainly shared that sentiment. As naked now as she was, he slid into the bed and put his arms around her, drawing her to him. Their mouths met in a heated kiss. Longarm parted her lips with his tongue and used it to explore her mouth, tasting the hot, wet sweetness of her. She reached down between them and closed her fingers around his shaft, which was already erect and throbbing with need. All of his tiredness and confusion and frustration had vanished. He was able to put it aside and live entirely in the here and now for a time, concerned only with sharing his passion with Claudette.

Neither of them was in any mood to wait. When he reached between her legs and probed her core with his fin-

131

gers, he found her drenched and ready for him. She rolled onto her back, spreading her thighs wide, and he moved over her and positioned himself to drive into her with a single urgent thrust. She gasped as his huge, rail-hard manhood filled her.

Her moisture coated his shaft as he moved it in and out of her. Her hips began to buck against him. She lifted her legs and wrapped them around him, locking her ankles together above his surging hips. Her arms twined around his neck and pulled his head down to hers, and once again their mouths molded together. He could feel her breasts flattened against his chest, the hard nipples prodding insistently against his bare skin.

The rhythm of their dance was timeless, universal. Longarm lost himself in her, driving his manhood deeper and deeper, reaching the inner core of her so that she gasped and cried out in ecstasy. Just as he could stand it no longer, she began to spasm around him, and thankfully he plunged deep within her one last time and held his shaft there as his own climax shook him. She shuddered and thrashed as his seed fountained into her, filling her to overflowing.

Longarm groaned as he collapsed onto her, barely able to support some of his weight with his elbows so that she could still breathe. Both of them were shiny with sweat. His pulse was hammering wildly in his head, like some mad carpenter building a gallows in Hell.

He frowned as that thought went through his head. Why in blazes had such a grim image sprung to mind at a time like this?

Then he heard something . . . a faint scraping . . . No, it was more like . . .

Slithering.

Longarm's head jerked up. Draped over the headboard of the bed was the biggest damn snake he had ever seen, and Longarm was practically eyeball to eyeball with it, so close that he could see its tongue flickering in and out of its mouth so fast that it was almost a blur.

Frozen there like that, he barely noticed when the door burst open behind him and the men with guns in their hands came into the room.

Chapter 13

Claudette looked up, saw the snake's head suspended in the air about twelve inches above her face, and quite understandably screamed like a banshee. Longarm's hand clamped over her mouth, cutting off the scream. He didn't want to spook the snake.

He had never heard of a snake this size being venomous; more than likely this was one of the creatures he had read about that killed its prey by looping its long, thick body around them and squeezing them to death. He had no idea how such a monster had gotten to New Orleans. They weren't native to this part of the country, or anywhere else in the United States, for that matter. He figured the men with the guns had something to do with it being in his hotel room, though.

"Do not move, M'sieu Parker," said one of the men. "We are sorry to interrupt you like this, but Marie Laveau wishes to see you."

The man's voice had the soft accent of the West Indies, and when Longarm risked a glance over his shoulder, he saw that the three unexpected visitors were black men wearing light-colored shirts and trousers and rope-soled sandals on their feet. Unlike the zombies, they were medium height and slender, but they were no less dangerous. They held their guns as if they knew quite well how to use them.

"I ain't going anywhere," grated Longarm, "until somebody does something about this damn snake."

"Pierre," said the man who had spoken before, and one of the other men tucked his pistol into his waistband and came forward. He reached out, grasped the snake's muscular body behind the head, and pulled it off the headboard. Some of the snake's body dropped onto the bed and slid across the pillow only inches from Claudette's head, and her eyes widened as another scream of instinctive horror tried to well up her throat. Longarm kept his hand over her mouth, blocking the sound. He didn't figure the gunmen would appreciate it if Claudette drew too much attention to them, and Longarm didn't want to give them any excuse to start shooting.

The snake draped itself around the torso of the man who was holding it. The man grinned and stroked the scaly flesh as if the snake was a pet cat.

"I am afraid we cannot do you the courtesy of turning around while you get dressed," said the spokesman. "We know that you are a resourceful man, M'sieu Parker. That is why the serpent was to visit you tonight."

"Let me guess," said Longarm. "You boys hid the snake in here earlier figuring it would crawl out and kill me after I went to bed. But then Marie Laveau decided she didn't want me dead after all, so she sent you back over here."

The spokesman inclined his head, acknowledging that Longarm's theory was correct. "Resourceful—and smart. After talking to the young lady, Madame Laveau decided she wishes to speak directly to you."

Longarm looked at Claudette, who seemed to have calmed down a little. At least she wasn't breathing quite as hard underneath him. He took his hand away from her mouth and said, "I reckon you saved my life by going to see the Voodoo Queen."

"That . . . that snake must have been under the bed the whole time!" she exclaimed with a shudder of revulsion.

"More than likely," agreed Longarm.

The leader of the gun-toting trio said, "Please get dressed now. Madame Laveau is waiting."

Longarm rolled off the bed and stood up. The gunmen watched him like hawks as he pulled on his underwear, trousers, and shirt. He had no chance to lunge toward the gunbelt lying on the bedside table. At least they had the decency to avert their eyes a little as Claudette got up and pulled on the gown she had worn at the Brass Pelican.

When Longarm had pulled on his socks and boots and Claudette had slid her feet into a pair of soft slippers, the leader of the gunmen said, "That is enough. We will go now."

"You plan on marching us out through the lobby at gunpoint with one of you carrying that snake?" Longarm asked dryly.

"We will go down the rear stairs. No one will hinder us. The bellmen who are on duty will see to that. They would not want to cause any inconvenience for Marie Laveau."

Longarm wasn't surprised by the answer. It was clear that Marie Laveau, the Voodoo Queen, wielded a great deal of power in New Orleans, even though she stayed in the shadows and pulled other people's strings like a master puppeteer. In a city filled with folks who believed in voodoo, the high priestess was someone to be feared and respected.

A few minutes later, Longarm and Claudette had been taken out through one of the hotel's rear doors into a service courtyard where a covered carriage waited. Black curtains were pulled over the carriage's windows. One of the gunmen opened the vehicle's door and gestured with his pistol for Longarm and Claudette to climb in. There was nothing else they could do.

Besides, Longarm wasn't really anxious to escape. After everything that had happened, he wanted to talk to Marie Laveau as much as she wanted to talk to him.

It was still not long after dawn as the carriage rolled through the streets of the French Quarter. Claudette huddled next to Longarm, clutching his arm nervously. Across from them sat two of the gunmen. The third man had placed the snake in a large wicker basket and climbed up on the seat of the carriage to ride next to the driver.

Longarm edged aside the black curtain on the window next to him. One of the Voodoo Queen's men lifted his gun, but Longarm held the palm of his other hand out toward the man, indicating that he wasn't going to try anything funny. He just wanted to see how the people on the street were reacting to the black carriage, and as he had expected, many of them turned their eyes away as soon as they glimpsed the grim-looking vehicle passing them.

"I reckon folks know this coach belongs to Marie Laveau," he commented to the two gunmen. "Most of 'em are pretending they don't even see it."

"Most people in New Orleans have a great deal of respect for Madame Laveau," said the gunman who had done all the talking so far. "You would be wise to do the same, M'sieu Parker."

Longarm nodded and let the curtain fall back into place. Voodoo powers aside, he had plenty of respect for anybody who could command men who handled guns and snakes so well.

The ride was not a long one. St. Anne Street ran from Jackson Square near the riverfront to Beauregard Square several blocks away. The carriage drew to a stop in front of a small, undistinguished cottage less than a block from Beauregard Square. As Longarm and Claudette climbed down, still under the guns of their captors, Claudette nodded toward the square, where most of the grass had been beaten away by the feet of generations, leaving hard-packed dirt behind. "Gran'pere's gran'mama told him of the dances the slaves held there," Claudette said in a low voice. "They call it Congo Square then. Gran'pere see the dance one time when he just a little boy. Say he never forget the drummin' and the chantin' and the singin'. That square a voodoo place, you bet.''

Longarm glanced at the open area, which looked innocuous enough in the early morning light, and still felt a chill as he thought about some of the things that might have happened there over all the lost decades.

"Move on," the leader of the gunmen ordered curtly. "No need for you to talk about such things."

They were touchy about their religion, thought Longarm, although according to what Claudette had told him, voodoo was really more of a bastard child of the original beliefs brought over to the West Indies by captured African slaves. He took Claudette's arm and led her up a narrow walk to the front door of the house. The two men followed them closely.

The door opened before Longarm and Claudette reached it. A pretty mulatto girl stood there, and she stepped back silently to let the visitors into the house. As Longarm entered the shadowy dwelling, a pungent, spicy smell came to him, not really unpleasant but quite distinctive. The girl who had let them in shut the door behind the two gunmen, who put their weapons away. Their attitude conveyed clearly the sense that guns were no longer needed.

They were in the presence of a power much greater than gunpowder and lead.

Moving noiselessly on bare feet, the girl led them down a corridor and into a room at the rear of the house. A fireplace with a large mantle stood on one side of the room, and despite the warmth of the morning, a fire was crackling merrily. The room was almost stifling with heat.

But the woman who sat in a large, straight-backed wooden chair near the fireplace was so old that she probably needed the flames to ward off the chill of the years. Longarm stopped, knowing that he was looking at Marie Laveau.

She was small, almost tiny, and made to look even more so by the size of the chair in which she sat. She wore a long gray dress and had a white lace shawl gathered around her

138

bony shoulders. Long white hair fell around her delicate head. Her skin was so pale she could have easily passed for white, and her bloodless pallor made her eyes seem that much darker. She had an air of frailty about her, but those eyes made all the difference in the world, thought Longarm. They shone with power and intelligence.

The girl who had brought them here went to stand just behind Marie Laveau's chair. Now that he could see both of them at the same time, Longarm noted a faint resemblance. The girl was probably Marie Laveau's great-granddaughter, he thought. Then, remembering what Claudette had told him about how far back the memory of the Voodoo Queen went, he revised that estimate and threw in a few more generations.

Marie Laveau spoke, her voice as thin and reedy as the wind. "You are the man called Custis Parker."

It wasn't a question, but Longarm nodded anyway. "Yes, ma'am, I reckon I am."

"But that is a lie," said Marie Laveau. "You are not the man you are pretending to be."

Longarm tried to conceal his surprise. How could this old woman know who he really was?

Unless she had read the truth in a pile of chicken entrails or something like that, a part of his brain yammered at him. He pushed those thoughts far back in his head and asked coolly, "Who do you think I am, ma'am?"

Marie Laveau shook her head. "I do not know . . . but I will. This one . . ." She raised her hand and pointed a claw-like finger at Claudette. "This one came to me on your behalf. I knew her gran'pere, and his gran'mama before him. I know the truth about *her*. And when she spoke to me of you, I knew that you had not told her the truth."

Claudette looked at Longarm in confusion. He was a mite mixed up himself. Maybe the best way to cut through all this would be to ask some direct questions.

"Did you send some men after me, ma'am? Men who some folks might call zombies?"

Longarm heard a hiss of indrawn breath from the men

behind him. Obviously, he was daring a lot by being so blunt with the Voodoo Queen.

Marie Laveau did not seem angered by the question. Instead, she nodded slowly and said, "I sent a man to find you. He had a restless spirit and asked this favor of me. His brother had been killed, and he wished revenge on the men he held responsible."

"Luther . . ." murmured Longarm, remembering the doorman at the Brass Pelican. His guess that the first zombie might have been Luther's brother had just been confirmed. But he was still puzzled. "Why would anybody blame me for Luther's death? I had just gotten to New Orleans when it happened."

"You went to work for him . . . for the evil one!"

"You mean Jasper Millard?"

Marie Laveau made a sharp gesture with a hand that was nothing but bone and skin like crepe paper. "Do not speak his name in this house. He has brought much pain and suffering to my people." She looked over Longarm's shoulder at the men who had brought him and Claudette here.

The one who had spoken before stepped forward and said in a low voice, "There are many West Indians here in New Orleans. Some are the descendants of slaves, while others came here since the end of the war. But all know the power of Marie Laveau, and it is to her they have come to tell of men and women who vanish mysteriously in the night."

Longarm looked over at the man. "Vanish?" he repeated. "You mean from some sort of magic spell?"

"I mean they are kidnapped and forced into slavery by evil men!"

Longarm drew a deep breath. "Well, if that don't beat all," he said slowly. "So that's what this is all about."

Claudette still looked confused. Hoping to clear up a few things for her—and get them straight in his own mind at the same time—he turned back to Marie Laveau and went on. "The fella you call the evil one, he's kidnapping folks here in New Orleans and shipping 'em back to the Caribbean

140

where their ancestors came from in the first place, isn't he? Slavery's still legal in some of those little island nations—like Saint Laurent."

Marie Laveau nodded solemnly.

"That's why Millard's men loaded that cargo on those ships of his in the middle of the night and didn't let the regular dockworkers near them," continued Longarm. "It was human cargo."

"Human cargo bound for the sugar plantation of the man who works with the evil one," said Marie Laveau.

"Paul Clement," Longarm said through gritted teeth. Clement was just as crooked as Millard, was in fact his business partner.

Longarm hoped that Annie wasn't in the scheme up to her pretty neck as well.

"Why come after me?" he asked. "Just because I work for . . . well, you know who I work for."

"You were to be brought here to me," explained the Voodoo Queen. "You would have been placed under my control and sent back to the evil one, so that we would know his plans."

"You were going to make a spy out of me. I'd've wound up a zombie."

What passed for a smile tugged briefly at the old woman's mouth. "It is a different spell, requiring different charms. But your ultimate fate would have been the same, once we were through with you. When our efforts did not go as planned, it was decided that you could best serve our purposes by dying, thereby robbing the evil one of a strong right hand."

"So you sent those fellas to put a giant snake in my room."

"Many creatures obey my commands," said Marie Laveau, "not merely those that are human."

"What made you change your mind?"

"This one," said Marie Laveau, pointing once again at Claudette. "As I told you, once I had spoken with her, I knew there was more to you than there appeared to be, M'sieu Parker. Now that you are here, I am more convinced than ever. You are not an evil man. Why have you allied yourself with one?''

Longarm took another deep breath. So much of the puzzle that he had found in New Orleans had been cleared up here in this unassuming little house by an old woman who looked like she would fall over if somebody breathed hard on her. Under the circumstances, he supposed it was time to tell the truth.

''I'm a United States deputy marshal,'' he said bluntly. ''My real name is Custis Long. I came to New Orleans to find out who was responsible for murdering another federal lawman who was trying to break up some smuggling rings.''

Claudette stared at him, wide-eyed with surprise. Marie Laveau merely nodded, as if his words came as no shock to her at all.

''The man in the bayou,'' she said. ''I heard of the fetish made to look like him which was placed outside the door of the chief marshal's office. It angered me greatly to think that someone would bring *voudun* into their petty criminal activities.''

''You and your folks didn't have anything to do with that?'' asked Longarm.

''Your law has nothing to do with us, we have nothing to do with it,'' said Marie Laveau. ''We wish only that the evil one be stopped.''

''Do you know someone named Royale?''

Once again that faint semblance of a smile appeared on Marie Laveau's gaunt face. ''I know the name,'' she said.

''Is Royale smuggling slaves back to the West Indies too?''

''The one you call Royale does nothing to harm my people. That is all I care about.''

Longarm wasn't sure why he believed the old woman, but he did. The friction between Royale and Millard was an added complication for him, but it had nothing to do with the voodoo angle. Which meant, he supposed, that the finger of guilt was pointing straight back at Millard again—and Paul Clement. Even though Millard professed to hate voodoo and want nothing to do with it, that didn't mean Clement felt the same way. Clement could have been the one responsible for placing the voodoo doll outside the chief marshal's office, in an attempt to muddy the waters and throw a false trail into any investigation of Douglas Ramsey's murder. The theory made sense, Longarm realized as he turned it over in his mind. The whole voodoo business had certainly had him guessing and coming up with some wild ideas, when once again, as usual, the motive all came down to money. He wondered how many other sugar plantations in the West Indies were being supplied with slave labor by Millard and Clement, and how high the price was.

But no matter how much those other plantation owners were paying, the price in human misery was even higher.

Marie Laveau steepled her bony fingers in front of her and asked, "What are you going to do about this matter?"

"I'm going to bust up that slavery ring good and proper," declared Longarm. "I'm convinced now that Mill—that the evil one and his partner are responsible for the murder of that other lawman. I'm going to call in some reinforcements and throw the whole lot of 'em behind bars."

"You can do this?" asked Marie Laveau.

Longarm thought about how that special prosecutor would react when he heard the password "Pikes Peak" and then Longarm laid this whole mess on his desk. He had a hunch Captain Denton and the other honest policemen in New Orleans would soon be paying a visit to the Brass Pelican and also to the Clement mansion on Chartres Street. Once again, he hoped that Annie's involvement in the affair had been slight or even nonexistent.

"I can do it," he promised Marie Laveau.

The Voodoo Queen nodded, evidently satisfied with his answer. "Then go. Put a stop to the evil one's crimes. But if you do not . . . then *I* will deal with him."

Jasper Millard didn't know it, thought Longarm, but he ought to be hoping right about now that the law caught up with him first.

Longarm clasped Claudette's hand as they were ushered out of the house and back into the carriage. "We will take you back to the hotel," said the leader of the gunmen, none of whom drew guns again now that they and Longarm seemed to be on the same side.

"Much obliged," said Longarm. He glanced over his shoulder one last time at the cottage. "That's a mighty scary old woman in there. No offense."

The man smiled thinly. "Only a fool would make an enemy of Marie Laveau."

"I reckon you've got that right, old son," Longarm said as he helped Claudette into the carriage.

Once Longarm and Claudette were rolling back through the streets toward the St. Charles Hotel—alone this time since the other men rode atop the carriage—Longarm lifted Claudette's hand and pressed his lips to the back of it. "Thank you," he murmured. "If the Voodoo Queen hadn't been so impressed with you, I'd still be in the dark about what was behind everything."

"I was so frightened, me," she said. "But I knew I would be all right as long as you were with me, Custis. If I had known you are a lawman—!"

"Sorry. I was keeping that under my hat until I got everything sorted out."

"You were nearly killed, you bet, because folks think that you were really workin' for Mr. Millard. Guess it's good I didn't stay at the Brass Pelican after all, me."

Longarm nodded. "Yeah, I'd say so. You can stay in my hotel room if you like, until I get everything cleared up. Then I'll take you back down to the bayou country, if that's what you want."

Claudette leaned back against the seat of the carriage and gave Longarm a wanton smile. "That would be most nice, I'm thinkin'." She grew more serious as she went on. "But

144

you be careful, you. Don't forget those men who try to kill you at the Mardi Gras parade last night.''

"Those were Royale's men," said Longarm. "They won't be a threat to me once I've arrested Millard and Clement and it's obvious I don't work for Millard anymore."

"You know that? You sure that this Royale send them after you?''

"Who else could have done it?''

"Somebody else who don't trust you, maybe?''

Longarm frowned. She was right, of course. He had just assumed that Royale had sent the would-be killers after him.

But maybe Millard had grown too suspicious after finding Longarm in his office and decided that it would be easier all around to get rid of his new employee—permanently.

"I reckon that'll all get sorted out too," said Longarm. "But I'll be careful, you can count on that.''

"You had better, or I come after you. I guarantee.''

They left the carriage in the courtyard behind the St. Charles and went in the way they had left, through the back door. There were no guns pointed at them this time, of course, and Longarm was thankful for that. Marie Laveau's men drove off with the carriage, and if he never saw them again, that would be perfectly all right with Longarm. He had had enough of snakes and zombies and voodoo. All that was left now was rounding up some good, old-fashioned crooks and killers.

Claudette sat down on the bed as Longarm buckled on his gunbelt. The mattress bounced a little underneath her, and the sound made Longarm think wistfully of what they had shared earlier. There was no time for a return engagement now.

But once Millard and Paul Clement were either behind bars or dead—depending on how they took to being arrested—then there would be plenty of time for Claudette.

He shrugged into his coat, bent over, and kissed her forehead. "I'll be back as soon as I can," he promised.

"Be careful," she said again. Her expression was taut with anxiety.

Longarm nodded, gave her a reassuring smile, and left the room. It had been a long time since he had slept or eaten anything, but he wasn't particularly tired or hungry. The anticipation of justice about to be served was its own fuel, he supposed, at least in his case. He walked quickly through the lobby and stepped out through the ornate front entrance onto the short flight of stairs that led down to the street.

A woman had just gotten out of a cab that was pulled up in front of the hotel, and as she hurriedly turned and started up the stairs, she stopped short. So did Longarm.

Annie Clement was staring up at him, and she looked scared to death.

Chapter 14

"Custis!" Annie exclaimed in a ragged voice. Then she rushed up the stairs toward him.

He caught hold of her arms and looked at her. She was wearing the same gown she had been wearing the night before at the Brass Pelican and the Mardi Gras parade. A small bruise discolored her left cheekbone, and her jaw had been scraped on that side as well. Someone had hit her.

Longarm led her along the steps well away from the doorman before he asked grimly, "What happened?"

"P-Paul," she gasped out. "He . . . he lost his temper with me . . . because I saw what he did last night."

"What do you mean?"

"At the Mardi Gras parade . . . I saw him point to you, and then a minute later, those men tried to kill you! I . . . I could not believe it. Paul grabbed my arm and took me away from there. I struggled against him, but it was no use." She leaned her head against Longarm's chest as a shudder went through her. "He . . . he took me back to the mansion, and when I demanded to know why those men tried to hurt you, he . . . he hit me."

"You didn't go back to the Brass Pelican after the ruckus at the parade?"

She shook her head. "No, we went straight to the house."

So Millard had lied to him, thought Longarm. That was yet another indication that Millard and Clement were the ones who had tried to have him killed. And it indicated as well how ruthless they were about not having their slave-smuggling scheme exposed. They had been willing to murder Longarm just on the off chance that he wasn't who he appeared to be.

"Did Paul tell you anything about why he wanted me dead?" he asked tautly.

Again Annie shook her head. "Only that it had to do with a business arrangement he has with Jasper Millard, and that I shouldn't ask any more questions."

"You don't know anything about that so-called business arrangement?"

"No. I swear, Custis, I don't. I . . . I thought they were just friends."

Longarm's expression was bleak as he asked, "What happened after Paul hit you?"

"He . . ." Annie swallowed hard. "He threw me on the bed in my room and . . . and took me."

Longarm's teeth grated together. "Your own brother?" he asked, horrified and furious.

She looked down and wouldn't meet his eyes. "He has been doing it for years."

Paul Clement was going to be damned lucky if he just wound up behind bars, thought Longarm. He wanted very much at that moment to put a bullet through the head of the sick, murderous son of a bitch and be done with it.

But as long as he was working for Uncle Sam he wasn't judge, jury, or executioner. He drew a tight rein on his emotions and said, "And after that?"

"He locked me in my room, as he often does. I finally managed to get out a window and reach a branch of the magnolia tree on that side of the house, so that I could climb down. I knew I had to find you, so I could warn you that Paul was trying to have you killed.''

"I'm obliged, but I already figured that out," he told her. "Your brother and Millard are partners in a smuggling ring, but it's not so much what they're bringing into the country that's got 'em worried about me. It's what they're shipping out."

"What?" asked Annie, a quaver of dread and apprehension in her voice.

Before Longarm could tell her, he heard rapid footsteps and the sound of a gun being cocked somewhere behind him.

He shoved Annie to the side as he whipped around, hoping that the push would send her out of the line of fire. A man in a tweed suit was standing behind one of the pillars that supported the hotel's second-floor balcony, using the pillar for cover as he aimed a Smith & Wesson revolver at Longarm. The weapon geysered flame and lead as an ugly whipcrack of sound split the early morning air. Longarm's gun was in his hand by now, and he heard the whine of the slug past his ear as he triggered his Colt.

Instinct and luck guided his shot. His bullet smashed the shoulder of the bushwhacker, knocking the man backward. The Smith & Wesson went flying.

That gunman wasn't the only threat, however, as Longarm saw right away. More men with drawn guns were darting from pillar to pillar, closing in on him and beginning to fire. At the same time, another cab drew up at the curb and several men leaped out of it, also with guns drawn. Clement must have discovered that Annie had escaped from the mansion and figured she would come looking for Longarm, and now he and Millard were desperate to get rid of both of them at the same time.

The doorman had ducked into the hotel for cover as shots rang out, but he was blowing his whistle frantically, the shrill sound keening through the air. That would summon the police, thought Longarm—but by the time help arrived, he and Annie would be dead, both of them shot full of holes.

Unless he did the unexpected.

Annie had slumped to the granite steps when Longarm shoved her, and so far she seemed to be unhit by the flying slugs. Longarm reached her side in a single bound and grabbed her arm, pulling her to her feet. He couldn't leave her behind. He snapped his last two shots at the men who had just emerged from the cab. The vehicle's driver, realizing how much danger he had innocently gotten mixed up in, was already whipping his horses into a run. As the gunmen ducked aside from Longarm's shots, the big lawman leaped down the steps toward the cab, hauling Annie with him.

He threw her bodily at the door of the cab, which was still flapping open as the driver pulled away from the curb. With a startled cry, Annie grabbed the door and pulled herself inside. Longarm leaped right behind her, but the door was already out of reach. The best he could do was catch onto the back of the cab with one hand while the other still held his Colt.

His arm felt as if it was nearly jerked out of its socket, but he managed to hang on. As he pulled his feet up, his body was thrown against the rear of the cab. The impact knocked the breath from his body, but still he held on. He jammed the empty Colt back in its holster, taking only a couple of tries to do so, then began clambering up the body of the cab.

Behind him, more shots blasted. Bullets thudded into the cab only inches from him. Longarm hoped the driver had the sense to swing around a corner as soon as they reached the end of the block. That would put them out of reach of the gunmen.

"Custis!"

The shout made him look up. Annie was hanging over the rear seat of the open-topped cab, extending a hand toward him. "Get down!" he called to her, but she shook her head stubbornly.

"Let me help you!" she cried over the rattle of the cab's wheels.

Figuring that it would be better not to waste time arguing, Longarm grasped her hand. At the same moment, he managed to finally get a foothold on the cab's body, and in a matter of seconds he pulled himself up and sprawled over the back of the seat, knocking Annie to the floor of the cab. Her face was white with fear, but she laughed hollowly at the awkwardness of it. Longarm was lying half on top of her. "This would be more enjoyable under other circumstances, Custis!" she said.

That was sure enough true. Longarm started to push himself up, then had to grab the side of the cab to catch his balance as the vehicle swayed at high speed around a corner. That was just what Longarm had hoped the driver would do. He raised his head for a last glance down the street in front of the hotel.

"Damn it!"

That glimpse had been enough to tell him that the men who were out for his scalp were piling into another cab, one they had stopped on the street at gunpoint. Longarm saw them jerking the cab's previous occupants and the driver out of the vehicle. One of the killers was going to handle the reins himself, more than likely. Then Longarm couldn't see any more, because the corner of the hotel cut off his view.

The gunmen weren't going to give up as easily as he had hoped. Longarm reached up and tapped the driver on the shoulder. The man cast a glance that was wide-eyed with fear at his unexpected passengers.

"Keep going as fast as you can!" shouted Longarm. "Head for the city hall! I'm a lawman!"

The driver bobbed his head and whipped the horses that much harder. Longarm was thrown against the rear seat as the cab lurched forward.

A bullet *spanged* off the metalwork beside him. "Look out, Custis!" screamed Annie.

Longarm swiveled his head and looked behind them. The other cab had taken the corner even tighter, and was now racing after them. He saw muzzle flashes from the guns of the men who worked for Clement and Millard. Since Annie was already sitting on the floorboard, he told her, "Stay down there!"

Looking forward again, he saw that the cab was approaching the riverfront. If the driver took a left when he reached the docks, that would bring them back to Decatur Street in a few blocks, and then they would reach the city hall within minutes. Longarm wanted to get Annie into the safety of the building and find that special prosecutor's office. There would be plenty of work for the man once Longarm laid out the story.

In the meantime, as he crouched on the floor of the cab next to Annie, he shucked the spent shells from his Colt and thumbed in fresh ones. Maybe he could slow down the pursuit, although he would have to be careful not to hit any pedestrians or other innocent bystanders along the street. Longarm raised himself up and lined the Colt's sights on the cab that was chasing them.

Before he could fire, a bullet sang past his ear, and he heard a grunt of pain. Annie screamed. Longarm jerked around, afraid that she had been hit. Instead, he saw that the driver of the cab was half-standing, clawing at his back where the bullet had caught him. With a groan, he toppled backward, landing upside down on the floorboards next to Annie. He was either unconscious or dead.

Longarm didn't have time to find out which, because the team pulling the cab was still running flat out—straight toward the Mississippi River.

Biting back a curse, Longarm clambered over the driver's body and scrambled over the front seat toward the driver's box. He looked desperately for the reins and saw them dangling over the front of the box. He made a frantic grab for them, but they slid out of his reach, falling under the hooves of the racing horses.

If someone didn't stop those animals or turn them aside, Longarm realized, they were going to run right into the river in about thirty seconds. He threw a glance back at the pursuers. They were still there, only they had closed the gap a little. Bullets were still thudding into the cab.

There was only one thing to do, Longarm told himself as the runaway cab crossed the street that ran alongside the river. The hooves of the horses thundered on the planks of a short dock as Longarm balanced himself and then leaped forward, intending to land on the back of one of the leaders so that he could at least use the harness to pull the team to a stop before the cab plunged into the river.

He was in midair before he realized that the attempt had come just a little too late. . . .

Then they were at the end of the dock and the horses and the cab were falling out from underneath him and he was falling too, and Annie was screaming and the waters of the mighty Mississippi came up and slammed into him, wrapping around him and pulling him down into the deepest darkness he had ever known in his life.

He was cold when he woke up, so cold that he thought he would never again be warm. The chattering of his teeth told him that he was still alive. A dead man couldn't feel like this—or so Longarm assumed. But then the thought struck him that maybe he was dead. Maybe what he was experiencing was the coldness of the grave.

And the fact that he was aware of the sensation meant that he was being brought back to a mere shambling semblance of life. He was being turned into a zombie!

The cry burst from his lips before he could stop it, and he heard an ugly chuckle from somewhere nearby. "Waking up, Parker—or whatever your name really is?"

The question came from Jasper Millard.

Someone else was close by. Longarm felt icy fingers clutching at his hand. The fingers of a corpse? No, they weren't that cold, he decided, and they had the strength and vitality of life as well.

"Custis! Please wake up, Custis. I thought you were dead."

Longarm's eyes fluttered open. "A-Annie?" he croaked out.

Her face swam into his line of sight, filling his vision as she leaned closely above him. Her hair was wild and damp, and there was a fresh bruise on her face. But she still looked beautiful to Longarm, because she was alive and that meant he was alive too.

The real question was how long that would hold true for each of them.

His vision had cleared enough for him to be able to look up past her and see a wooden roof high overhead. As she babbled her gratitude that he was still among the living, her voice echoed hollowly, and Longarm realized now that Millard's words had had a definite echo too. They were in a large room somewhere—not the Brass Pelican, Longarm decided. Someplace else.

"I think we should just go ahead and shoot him right here and now. He's bound to be a lawman."

That was Millard's voice again, booming out its threat. Someone answered him in a smoother, more sophisticated tone. "No, it will be much more effective to feed him to the alligators. Perhaps part of his body will be found too, and send a message to the authorities." Paul Clement, thought Longarm. That son of a bitch.

"Yeah, like we sent a message with that other badge-toting snooper? It was bad enough that all of his corpse didn't get eaten, but then you had to go and leave that voodoo doll on his boss's doorstep. I don't like messing with that voodoo shit, and besides, it just stirred up the law that much more."

"I believed it would confuse the issue enough to throw off any investigation into Ramsey's death," Clement replied coldly. "I did what I thought was best, Jasper—and you should remember whose idea our arrangement was in the first place."

"Yeah, yeah," replied Millard in a surly tone. "You're a damn genius, all right."

"I've made us a great deal of money so far. The other plantation owners on Saint Laurent and the neighboring islands are quite happy to meet our price for the workforce we provide."

Their squabbling had confirmed all of Longarm's speculations and answered all the questions that had brought him to New Orleans. The knowledge wasn't going to do him a hell of a lot of good, though, unless he could somehow get away from his captors and find some help.

While Millard and Clement were talking, Annie had been stroking Longarm's face and huddling against him in fear. He was aware now that he was soaking wet and lying on a hard floor. Probably no more than half an hour had passed since the runaway cab had plunged into the river; based on that fact, the high ceiling, the shadows that filled the big room, and the likely proximity to the riverfront, he figured they were in a warehouse. Millard probably owned at least one such building, so that he could store the goods he smuggled into New Orleans until he had a chance to dispose of them.

A warehouse would be a good place to hold prisoners who were destined to be shipped out to the West Indies and a life of slavery on the sugar plantations too. Longarm wondered if there were any such captives here now, or if he and Annie were the only prisoners.

There was only one way to find out. His hands weren't tied, he realized, so he got them under him and pushed himself into a sitting position.

"Don't try anything, Marshal," warned Clement. "You *are* a United States marshal, I take it."

"Custis Long," admitted Longarm. "I'd show you my badge and bona fides, but I left 'em back in Denver."

"Ah, they sent in a man all the way from Colorado, just so that no one here would recognize you. Quite a plan." Clement's tone was mocking.

"Yeah, and it worked too," said Longarm dryly. "All you bastards are under arrest."

Clement laughed, but Millard just glowered at Longarm. The two partners in crime were standing about a dozen feet away. They were flanked by four gunmen, no doubt some of the assassins who had been sent after Longarm and Annie at the hotel. The men had their weapons drawn and ready, so even though Longarm's hands and feet were not tied, there was no way he could make a move against Clement and Millard.

The warehouse was perhaps half full of crates of various shapes and sizes. There was probably all kinds of contraband hidden here, thought Longarm. He wondered if there was anything around he could use for a weapon. Faint light filtered in through small, filthy windows that were set high in the walls just under the ceiling. A couple of kerosene lanterns that had been placed on crates also provided illumination.

To stall for time, and to satisfy his own curiosity, Longarm asked, "Why did your men pull us out of the river instead of letting us drown? From the looks of things, you wanted us both dead anyway, so you could've let the Mississippi take care of it for you."

"I was nearby, keeping an eye on things," replied Clement, "and when I saw that cab go into the water, I put in an appearance and ordered the men to rescue you and Annie. Then we brought you here because I have an even more appropriate fate in mind for you both."

"Yeah, I heard," grunted Longarm. "You plan on feeding me to the gators. Is that what you're going to do to your own sister?" Beside him, Annie grew even paler, and her hands tightened on his arm.

"Of course not," said Clement with a shake of his head. "Jasper here got worried when he found you snooping in his office, so he decided that the best thing to do would be to get rid of you, even though you might have been telling the truth about wanting one of those Cuban cigars. I concurred. We can't afford to take any chances of our operation being discovered by the law. Then poor Annie realized that we were trying to have you killed after that donnybrook at the

156

Mardi Gras parade, and she became quite upset. I had to take stern measures to calm her down.''

"You *raped* me!'' Annie hissed at him. "The same way you've been raping me for years, ever since I was fourteen years old! How could you? I'm your sister, you . . . you . . .'' Hatred and horror made words fail her.

Smiling, Clement slid one of the Cuban cigars from his vest pocket and sniffed it appreciatively. "Hardly,'' he said. "You were never told about it, my dear, but our parents merely adopted you when you were only an infant. You're not a blood relation at all, so I saw no reason not to avail myself of your charms.'' His fingers tightened on the cigar as venom began to drip from his words. "As a matter of fact, you're an octoroon, darling Annie. You have nigger blood flowing in your veins.'' Clement controlled himself with a visible effort, stuck the cigar in his mouth, and said around it, "So I've decided to send you to one of the other islands so that you can work in the fields with the other niggers.''

"You . . . you . . .'' Again, Annie could not find the words to convey her loathing of the man she had considered her brother.

"Son of a bitch?'' suggested Longarm. "Low-down rabid skunk? No, I reckon that'd be an insult to the skunk.''

Clement shook his head and said, "Go ahead and have your fun, Marshal. You're going to be dead very soon anyway.''

"Yeah,'' put in Millard. "And you were a piss-poor right-hand man. Sure, you helped out a little those times Royale tried to get at me, but I could've just as easily been killed.''

"What about Royale?'' asked Longarm, again trying to postpone his impending death. "What's his part in all of this?''

"Just what I already told you,'' said Millard. "He runs another smuggling ring, and he wants to put me out of business.''

"Does he run slaves to the West Indies too?''

157

Millard shook his head and snorted in contempt. "Not that I've ever heard. He may be a murdering, cold-blooded bastard, but he's too good to get his hands dirty with something like slave-running."

That just about wrapped it up, thought Longarm. Royale's activities and the involvement of the Voodoo Queen had been mere distractions in this case, despite the dangers they had represented. Almost from the moment of his arrival in New Orleans, he had been right in amongst the very men he was after. Clement's part in the smuggling scheme, and in Douglas Ramsey's murder, had been unexpected, but Jasper Millard was indeed a villain, just as Longarm had suspected from the beginning.

Clement drew a small pistol from his pocket. "Now, Marshal Long," he said, "I believe you have an appointment with some scaly friends of ours."

Annie pushed herself in front of Longarm. "No!" she cried out. "You can't do this, Paul." Her tone softened. "If . . . if I ever meant anything to you, I'm asking you to spare us—"

Clement leveled and cocked his weapon. Beside him, Millard also drew a gun, and the other four men raised theirs. "Oh, you meant something to me, all right," he said to Annie, "but not nearly as much as the money does. And I'll simply shoot you too unless you get out of the way."

Longarm saw that he was going to have to shove Annie aside, out of the line of fire, and then come up off the floor in a desperate lunge at Clement and Millard. He'd be shot full of holes before he got halfway there, he knew, but at least making such a play might save Annie's life.

Though what sort of life it would be, condemned to slavery, was another matter entirely. . . .

Longarm's muscles were tensed and he was ready to move, but he didn't have to.

Because behind Clement and Millard, the huge wooden double doors that led into the warehouse suddenly blew up with no warning.

Chapter 15

The explosion shattered the doors, sending a hail of flame, noise, and splinters into the warehouse. Clement and Millard were thrown forward as if a giant hand had slapped them on the back. Their gunmen were staggered too. A couple of them cried out as large splinters of wood from the doors sliced their hands and faces.

Longarm grabbed Annie and threw both of them flat on the floor, shielding her with his body. The force of the explosion and the debris that it flung out passed over them, leaving them unharmed. Longarm barked, "Stay down!" in Annie's ear, then levered himself up off the planks of the floor. He put all the momentum of his movements behind the punch he threw at Paul Clement.

His fist smashed into Clement's jaw so hard that Longarm felt a satisfying shiver all the way up his arm to the elbow. Clement's head slewed around and his knees came unhinged. Longarm made a grab for the pistol as Clement fell, but it slipped out of Clement's hand and bounced away across the floor.

Longarm saw Millard's mouth working and read the bald

man's lips. *Kill them! Kill them!* But he heard only muffled sounds because he was half-deafened by the explosion. He realized that Annie might not have heard his order to stay down, and when he turned his head to check on her safety, something crashed into him. As he fell, the hands of the man who had just tackled him closed around his throat, cutting off his air.

That sensation brought back memories of almost being killed by the first so-called zombie who had come after him, Luther's brother, whom Longarm had been forced to kill. This man was no zombie, just a hired ruffian, and Longarm was able to loosen his grip by bringing a knee up into his groin. He felt that, all right. Longarm brought his cupped hands up and slapped them over the man's ears. He howled in pain and let go, and Longarm was able to heave him off to the side.

Longarm rolled over and came up on hands and knees, and as he did so, he saw a wagon burst out of the smoke hanging in the opening that had been blown in the wall. The horses pulling it were wild-eyed from the smoke and the noise of the blast. Or maybe they were just Hell-horses, Longarm thought crazily, because the men who clambered down from the wagon sure enough looked like denizens of Hades.

They were huge, and Longarm had to ask himself if their eyes were actually glowing or if it was just a trick of the light. Their slow, awkward movements were familiar to Longarm, as was the way they jerked but did not fall from the bullets fired by the gunmen. Clearly, the explosion and this attack were presents from the Voodoo Queen.

Longarm could wonder how Marie Laveau had known of the danger he and Annie were in later, after things had settled down. For the moment, he was still concerned with keeping the two of them alive, and the best way to do that was to remove the threat of Clement and Millard.

From the corner of his eye, Longarm saw one of the men from the wagon grab hold of a gunman. The hired killer shrieked and emptied his pistol into the man's chest, but the effect of the shots was too late to save him. The death blow was already falling. The man's balled fist came hammering down on the gunman's head, crushing his skull like an egg-shell. Longarm's hearing was starting to come back, and he could have sworn that he heard the crunch of bone. Slowly, both men toppled over, dead before they hit the floor.

Longarm scooped up the pistol Clement had dropped and swung around toward Millard. A desperate look was on Millard's face as he shouted, "Scott! Willie!" at the two remaining henchmen who were still on their feet. Scott and Willie had problems of their own, however, and couldn't come to his help. Both of them were trying to avoid the lunges of the zombies who were after them.

Millard grimaced and pegged a shot toward Longarm. The bullet whipped past Longarm's head as he returned fire. Millard was already darting aside, and Longarm's shot missed. Millard threw himself toward the piles of crates, intending to use them for cover. Longarm ran after him.

Millard knew the layout of the warehouse a lot better than *he* did, Longarm realized. Once Millard got in that maze of stacked-up boxes, he would be as difficult to track down as a rat in a hole. Longarm snapped another shot at him, then grated a curse as he saw the slug kick up splinters from the crate behind which Millard had just disappeared.

"Custis!" Annie cried out behind him.

He jerked around to see that she was on her feet, pointing toward the other side of the warehouse. One of the gunmen was dangling limply by the neck from the hands of one of the Voodoo Queen's men, but the other one was still struggling with his almost inhuman opponent as flames danced around their feet. Longarm saw the shattered chimney of a lantern shining in pieces on the floor near them, and knew that in their struggle they must have jostled it off the crate on which it had been sitting. The kerosene that had spilled when the lantern broke had ignited furiously, and now the flames were spreading rapidly across the floor to more of the crates.

Longarm cast a glance over his shoulder toward the spot where Millard had vanished. There was no time to try to root him out now. Instead, Longarm ran across the big room toward Annie. As he reached her, he saw the broken body of the final gunman being cast aside. The zombie shambled a couple of steps as if confused, then stopped and sank to his knees. His shirt was sodden with blood, the spreading stain black in the harsh glare of the flames. He pitched slowly forward onto his face, and then lay still as death claimed him. Longarm realized that he and Annie were the only ones still on their feet.

He grabbed her arm and hustled her over toward the wagon. The horses were trying to rear up in their traces, driven mad by the smoke and the smell of blood. Longarm helped Annie up into the bed of the wagon, then ran back for the one gunman who was still alive, the one who had been trying to choke Longarm to death until he had busted the man's eardrums. Longarm saw trails of blood leading out of both ears as he stooped to grab the unconscious man under the arms and drag him toward the wagon. Deaf or not, he could still testify against Clement and Millard.

Longarm hoisted the man and threw him into the back of the wagon. Annie cringed away from him. Longarm turned back for Clement and realized angrily that the mastermind behind the slave-running scheme was gone. "What the hell!" Longarm exclaimed aloud. Only moments ago, Clement had been lying right there on the floor where he had fallen after Longarm knocked him out . . . hadn't he?

Longarm didn't know. In the noise and confusion, almost anything could have happened and he might not have noticed. What mattered now was that he was running out of time. One entire wall of the warehouse was already ablaze, and the flames were spreading toward the jagged opening where the doors had been.

There was no sign of Millard either. Longarm didn't know

if he had gotten out of the building by some other way or was still somewhere in those small mountains of crates. Being careful that he didn't get anywhere near the lashing hooves of the horses, Longarm hurried to the front of the team and reached up to grab the harness of one of the leaders. It took all of his strength to haul the animal back down and bring it under some semblance of control. Straining and pulling, he led the team in a circle until they were pointed back toward the opening.

"Hang on!" Longarm shouted to Annie, then he slapped the closest of the leaders on the rump as hard as he could and jumped back out of the way.

With the sight and smell of open air in front of them, the horses lunged forward, pulling the wagon behind them. Longarm saw Annie holding tightly to one of the sideboards as the vehicle rocked and clattered out through the opening. Longarm cast one more look around the inside of the warehouse, making certain that everyone else was dead. There was still no sign of Clement or Millard.

Longarm ran out into the fresh air after the wagon. It was an overcast day, but the sunlight that made it through the clouds still seemed almost painfully bright after the dimness of the warehouse. Longarm saw a crowd of dockworkers converging on the burning warehouse, and somewhere in the distance he heard bells clanging. The fire wagons would be here soon.

He gulped down deep breaths of air, and despite the humid stickiness and the rotten fish odor, nothing had ever smelled quite as good to him. When he looked back at the building, thick gouts of black smoke were billowing up from the warehouse, filling the sky above the Crescent City and the mighty river that ran through it. The roof was blazing now, and with a roar, part of it fell in. All the contraband Clement and Millard had stored there was going to be consumed in the fire.

The thought of Clement and Millard made a bitter taste clog Longarm's mouth. The two ringleaders had gotten

163

away. They were responsible for the murder of a federal lawman, as well as untold suffering on the part of the men and women who had been kidnapped and forced into slavery. Add to that the suffering of the loved ones left behind by those victims of the slavery ring, and the toll was high.

Longarm was not going to rest until Clement and Millard had paid for it.

One of the dockworkers came running up to him and grasped his arm. "Hey, mister, you all right?" asked the man. When Longarm managed to nod, the dockworker went on. "What in hell happened?"

"Hell," murmured Longarm, but it wasn't a curse. "You're closer to right than you know, old son."

Longarm turned away from the man, who had a confused expression on his face, as a woman called urgently, "Custis!" The voice didn't belong to Annie Clement, though. When Longarm turned around, he saw Claudette hurrying through the crowd toward him.

She threw herself into his arms and kissed him. Instinctively, Longarm embraced her, pulling her close against him. After a moment, Claudette moved her head back, breaking the kiss, and asked anxiously, "You are all right, you?"

"I'm fine," he assured her. "A mite wet and bedraggled and beat up, but you can bet I'll live."

"When I saw from the window of the hotel room, me, how those men were shooting at you, I knew I had to help you. So I pulled my clothes on and took myself off through the back of the hotel mighty quicklike, and I went to see Marie Laveau."

"How'd you know where to tell her to find me?" asked Longarm, puzzled.

Claudette shook her head. "Marie Laveau, she got her ways of findin' anybody she want to. An' so do I."

The answer didn't satisfy him, but Longarm let it pass for the moment. The important thing was that he and Annie was still alive, thanks to Claudette. Not only that, but several of the men who had been working for Clement and Millard were dead, and the two schemers themselves were now on the run. Their stranglehold on the West Indians who lived in New Orleans was broken.

With an arm around Claudette, Longarm went over to the wagon, which had come to a halt a safe distance from the burning warehouse. Annie was still sitting in the back of the vehicle, looking half-stunned. Near her, the man Longarm had tossed into the wagon was stirring around as consciousness came back to him. Longarm turned to a couple of the curious bystanders and pointed to the man. "I'm a United States deputy marshal," he told the onlookers. "Grab that fella and hang on to him until the local law gets here. He's under arrest."

The men were only too eager to help, even though Longarm hadn't flashed a badge or any other identification at them. They climbed into the wagon and found some rope, which they promptly used to truss up the prisoner.

Meanwhile, Longarm stepped up onto the driver's box and leaned over the back of the seat to hold out a hand to Annie, who was still huddled against the sideboard. "Come on, Annie," he said. "Let's get you out of there."

She looked up at him, hollow-eyed with shock, but after a moment her gaze cleared a little and she was able to nod. She reached up and clasped Longarm's hand. He lifted her to her feet and helped her down from the wagon.

Claudette stood nearby, watching curiously, and over the clanging of the bells from the fire wagons that were approaching, she said, "Mademoiselle Annie is all right?"

"She will be," said Longarm. "With any luck, she will be."

The fire wagons raced by and came to a stop in front of the warehouse, but it was evident that nothing could save the building now. More than half of it had already been consumed by the inferno. The concern now was to keep the flames from spreading to the surrounding structures, and the firemen joined their efforts with those of the bucket brigade that had already formed to wet down the other buildings.

With the river so close by, there would be no shortage of water for the tanks on the fire wagons.

Men were running around and shouting, but even in that confusion, Longarm heard someone bellow, "*Parker!*" Only one man would still be calling him that out of habit, Longarm thought as he jerked around and looked toward the burning warehouse in time to see something that would remain etched in horror on his brain for a long time to come.

A figure lurched out of the fire-filled opening in the wall, and even though flames flickered all around it, the blazing form managed to keep moving. Longarm recognized the human torch as Jasper Millard, and knew that Millard must have tried to get out of the warehouse by some other means, only to fail and be trapped in the blaze.

Annie and Claudette were flanking Longarm, and both of them gasped and cried out. Millard's shambling gait reminded Longarm of the zombies, but no potion or black magic ritual was animating the man's body. Millard was moving and staying alive through the power of sheer hate, and as he stumbled toward Longarm the firemen and the crowd of dockworkers and onlookers fell back, just as horrified as Longarm and the two women were.

Somehow, Millard managed to keep coming until he was only a dozen feet away from Longarm. The flames surrounding him had died out, leaving behind only a blackened, crackling husk of a man. Millard raised his hands and lurched toward Longarm, the bones of his fingers showing through the burned flesh.

Then Longarm raised the pistol he still held in his hand and said, "I'd tell you to burn in Hell, Millard, but I reckon you're already there."

The whipcrack of the pistol shot shattered the eerie silence that had fallen. Millard's head jerked back as the bullet bored through a brain that had already boiled in its own fluids. One more stumbling step, and Millard collapsed. Longarm almost expected him to fall apart in ashes when he hit the street, but the charred corpse remained intact. Longarm slowly lowered the gun as more flames and smoke rose from the burning warehouse.

"Drop that gun, mister!"

The order came from behind Longarm, roared in a harsh voice. Before he turned, Longarm leaned over and placed the gun on the ground, then straightened and swung around to face a furious Captain Denton of the New Orleans police force. The captain's face was brick-red with anger.

"Damn it, I just saw you murder that man!" burst out Denton.

"I'd call it putting him out of his misery—and ours," said Longarm.

"I don't care what you call it, you're under arrest!" Denton gestured to the blue-uniformed men with him. "Take this man into custody!"

A tired grin plucked at Longarm's mouth. "I'll go peaceablelike, Captain, especially if you'll take me to see the special prosecutor."

Denton frowned in confusion. "What in blazes are you talking about?"

"I've got a story to tell that fella . . . all about Pikes Peak."

Chapter 16

Saint Laurent rose green and beautiful from the waters of the Caribbean, an island some twenty miles long and ten wide, its eastern end dominated by a rugged volcanic peak that had long since become inactive. From the mountain, the land sloped gradually to the west in a series of gentle hills and broad valleys filled with stalks of sugarcane. Along the western shore was a sandy beach dotted with clumps of palm trees. It was a truly lovely place, thought Longarm as he stood at the railing of the ship that had brought him here, his hands gripping it tightly.

Too bad Saint Laurent had such ugliness hiding amidst its beauty.

A week had passed since the fire that had consumed the warehouse used by Paul Clement and Jasper Millard to house the goods they smuggled into the country—and sometimes those they smuggled out. Longarm had spent a goodly portion of that week explaining things first to Captain Denton, then to a series of the captain's superiors, culminating in that special prosecutor whose summons had brought Longarm to New Orleans in the first place. Then there had been the flurry of telegraph messages burning up the wires between the Crescent City and the Mile High City as Longarm attempted to clear everything up for Billy Vail. None of it had been easy, but finally everyone involved had accepted Longarm's explanations, and Vail had ordered him to return to Denver.

Longarm didn't like disobeying a direct order, but he had done it before when it was necessary, and this was one of those times.

Paul Clement's body had not been found in the burned-out warehouse, which meant that he had regained consciousness and slipped out of the building before the fire spread, while Longarm had his hands full with other matters. Clement had raped Annie—and even though she had been adopted, Longarm still considered that incest—and he had been responsible for plenty of other evil doings.

As long as Clement was walking around free and breathing perfectly good air, Longarm wasn't going back to Denver.

Avoiding Billy Vail's orders had necessitated a bribe out of Longarm's own pocket to a telegraph operator in New Orleans. The key-pounder had sent back a wire saying that there was trouble along the line and to please repeat the last message, and Longarm had lit a shuck out of that Western Union office and headed for the hotel, then the docks.

Luck had been with him, and within an hour, he was on a ship sailing for Saint Laurent. The vessel had other ports of call in the West Indies, but Saint Laurent was the only one in which Longarm was interested.

The captain of the ship came up and leaned on the railing beside Longarm. "Are you sure you want us to put you ashore here, Marshal?" asked the man. "There's a good-sized port city just down the coast a few miles."

"This'll do fine, as long as it's not too much trouble for you and your men, Captain," replied Longarm.

"All right," the captain said with a shrug. "I'll have the men lower a boat, and we'll have you safely ashore in a few minutes."

Longarm supposed that making this voyage had been in

the back of his mind from the very moment he had discovered that Paul Clement had not perished in the burning warehouse. He had gotten hold of a map of Saint Laurent and sat down with Annie so that she could show him where the Clement sugar plantation was located. Longarm tried to keep the conversation light and innocuous, but he thought he could see awareness in Annie's eyes. She wanted him to go after Paul too.

Claudette had not been quite so understanding. When he had stopped by the St. Charles to throw a few things into his warbag, she had caught hold of his arm and looked up at him worriedly.

"Custis, you are not leaving yet, no," she had insisted.

"Afraid I've got to," Longarm had told her. "There's something left undone."

"You are not responsible for bringing justice to the whole world, you."

"I'm responsible for my part of it."

"But Custis . . ." And here she had lowered her voice and come into his arms, reaching down to slide her hand over his groin and then cup his shaft, which was growing hard despite his best intentions. "There is so little-little time, and so much we have not done, us."

"Maybe I'll be back to New Orleans someday," Longarm had told her in a husky whisper.

She had turned away from him and flounced across the room. "An' maybe I will not be here, me."

That was how they had left things, and even now, Longarm felt like sighing in regret as he climbed down into the small boat that would take him ashore on Saint Laurent. Claudette was one hell of a woman.

But when you came right down to it, he had ultimately said good-bye to every woman he had ever met. That was part of the price of carrying a badge. Other lawmen might be able to marry and have families, but Longarm had never figured he could manage it. The chances were too good he would leave a widow behind, probably with a passel of kids who would miss their daddy something fierce. The bitter-sweet pain of always saying good-bye was easier to bear.

At least he hadn't had to say good-bye to Marie Laveau. He had only seen the Voodoo Queen that one time, and if he never crossed trails with her again, that would be just fine with him.

The small boat's hull scraped the sand of the beach, and one of the crewmen jumped out to pull it higher out of the water. Longarm stood up carefully, his warbag thrown over his shoulder, and stepped out onto the sand. "Much obliged, gents," he said to the men who had brought him ashore.

The second mate, who commanded this detail, said, "The cap'n told me to tell you, Marshal, that we'll be in port down the coast for a day, if you want to catch up to us once your business is taken care of."

Longarm nodded. "I'll sure try to do that, old son. Reckon you've got room for another passenger besides me?"

"Plenty of room in the brig," said the young sailor with a grin.

Longarm returned the grin and touched a finger to the brim of his hat as the boat was pushed off. The sailors didn't know exactly what had brought him to Saint Laurent, but they had a pretty good idea. They had figured out that he hoped to have a prisoner with him on the return voyage.

Longarm hoped so too. Paul Clement deserved to spend some time behind bars—before he wound up at the end of a hangman's rope.

The closest Longarm had ever been to the tropics was the jungles of southern Mexico. The thick vegetation here along the coastline of Saint Laurent was similar, and so were the prevalent smells of rich earth and decay. He pushed through the clinging plants and walked inland, watching for snakes and other varmints. He almost wished he had a machete, so that he could chop an easier path through the jungle. Even an old-fashioned Bowie knife would have come in handy.

Luckily, though, he didn't have far to go. By late afternoon, he had reached the edge of the fields that were planted with sugarcane. It would be a while before the crop was ready for harvesting, but the stalks were already pretty tall. Longarm was grateful for their concealment as he hunkered down among them and waited for the sun to go down.

He would wait for nightfall before he paid a visit to Paul Clement.

Somewhere far off in the darkness, a jungle cat of some sort let out a howl. Longarm grimaced. Back in his usual stomping grounds, such a sound would have come from a wolf or a coyote or maybe even an Apache on the prowl. Here on this tropical island, he didn't know what sort of big cats might be wandering around.

He glanced up at the sky overhead, black as sable and dotted with pinpricks of brilliant light. He would be glad when he was once more under the light of Western stars.

About fifty yards from where Longarm crouched, the plantation house belonging to Paul Clement loomed in the middle of a clearing that had been hacked out of the jungle. A broad veranda ran all the way around the house, and several tall, broad-shouldered men carrying rifles patrolled it regularly. Longarm had been able to establish that much after spying on the house for only a few minutes. As one of the guards turned a corner, another rounded the far corner, so that each side of the house always had a sentry watching for trouble. Getting in there was going to be a challenge—and he wasn't even sure that Paul Clement was inside, although it seemed likely considering the way the place was guarded.

And there was really nowhere else Clement could have gone. The police in New Orleans had searched the mansion on Chartres Street and found no sign of him. Officers had been left on duty there in case he returned. But Longarm thought it was much more likely—and Annie agreed with him—that Clement had run back home to Saint Laurent. Though his schemes had been ruined, here in this stronghold he could live out the rest of his life without being disturbed.

Or so he thought. Longarm didn't intend to let that happen.

A door leading onto the veranda opened, and a man stepped out to speak in low tones to the guard who was patrolling that side of the house at the moment. Slender, dressed in immaculate white trousers and a blousy white shirt, the man was undoubtedly Paul Clement. Longarm's jaw tightened as he watched Clement talking to the guard. The big man nodded, and Clement went back inside.

A couple of minutes later, two more men came from the direction of the slave quarters. They had a young black woman with them. The dress she wore was short and so tight that her lush body seemed to be on the verge of bursting out of it. She looked scared and reluctant, and Longarm wasn't surprised when she was taken up on the veranda and led into the house. Clement had almost certainly sent for her so that she could warm his bed tonight.

Longarm's fingers strayed to the walnut grips of the Colt he carried in his cross-draw rig. He was no cold-blooded killer, and he wasn't just about to take the law into his own hands . . . but a man like Clement made him at least ponder the possibility for a few moments before discarding it.

If he could, Longarm was going to take Clement back to New Orleans so that the law could deal with him. But if Clement made that impossible . . . well, Longarm wasn't going to lose a hell of a lot of sleep over it. Or *any* sleep, for that matter.

It was going to take a distraction for him to be able to get into the house, Longarm realized. But what was it going to be?

The sudden shouts that came to his ears through the warm night air made his head jerk up. He looked around, toward the slave quarters. An orange glow lit the sky in that direction, and even though Longarm didn't speak much French, he knew that whoever was hollering over there was alerting the plantation to the fact that something was on fire.

Providence, thought Longarm. He looked toward the house and saw that the other three guards had run around the veranda to join the one on this side. All four of the sentries were staring toward the slave quarters.

Clement appeared in the doorway behind them, his shirt open to the waist. He yelled at them in French and waved a hand toward the fire. Three of the four sentries took off in a run, and passed within ten feet of where Longarm was hidden at the edge of the path. None of them saw him.

As he had back in New Orleans, Longarm thought about luck and how he basically distrusted it. But since nobody knew he was here, this couldn't be a trap for him, and besides, he doubted that even somebody as ruthless as Clement would burn down the slave quarters just to bait a trap.

No, this was an opportunity Longarm had to take advantage of, and he intended to do just that.

He began circling the house, working his way through the brush. He didn't know the names of most of these tropical plants, but they were persistent in clinging to him. Not wanting to make much noise, he couldn't hurry, but even so, within a few minutes he reached a spot where the sole remaining sentry couldn't see him. Longarm drew his gun, emerged from the undergrowth in a crouch, and sprinted across the clearing toward the plantation house.

When he reached the veranda, he slowed and stepped up carefully, rather than bounding. Silence was still important, although judging by the shouts in the night, none of the other sentries were paying attention to anything except the fire. Longarm glanced in that direction again and decided it wasn't the slave quarters that were burning after all. The blaze that lit up the night sky was too big for that.

It looked to him like the cane fields were on fire. . . .

If that was the case, then no wonder Clement was so upset that he had sent all but one of his guards away to help battle the blaze. The sugarcane was all he had left to help him recoup his losses from the destruction of the slave-running ring.

Longarm cat-footed along the wall to the nearest door and

carefully tried the knob. It was locked, which came as no surprise. Maybe one of the windows . . .

Each of them that Longarm tried was latched as well. He didn't have time to go around the entire house trying all the doors and windows. He had to get inside more quickly than that.

He went to the edge of the veranda. There was a railing around it, and it took only a moment to step up on that railing and reach up to the edge of the roof that overhung it. Longarm had to holster the gun so that he could use both hands, but he was able to swing up onto the roof of the veranda without much trouble. Maybe one of the windows on the second floor wouldn't be fastened.

He saw right away in the moonlight that none were. In fact, one of them stood wide open so that the night breezes could flutter the thin white curtains that hung inside it. Longarm slid the Colt from its holster once more as he moved to the window. The room inside was dark, and no sound came from it. Longarm swung a leg over the sill and dropped through the window.

He landed on something soft—something that let out a muffled cry and then started flailing away at him furiously.

Longarm figured out what had happened and lifted an arm to ward off the blows. "Stop it!" he hissed. "I'm here to help you! Settle down, damn it!"

The whispered words got no response, so he had no choice but to grab the figure struggling with him. She was young and lithe and naked, and he didn't have to be a genius to figure out that she was the same young woman who had been taken reluctantly into the house to serve as a plaything for Paul Clement. He managed to get hold of both her wrists with one hand and found himself sitting astride her on a four-poster bed. "Hush!" he said quickly as he heard her draw a deep breath in preparation for a scream. "I'm the law, and I've come for Clement!"

That wasn't strictly true. He was a hell of a long way from anywhere where he had jurisdiction. But he meant to bring

Paul Clement to justice anyway. That fact must have penetrated the young woman's brain, because she stopped struggling. After panting for a moment, she said, "M'sieu Clement . . . is an evil man."

"Don't I know it," said Longarm.

"You are here to . . . to kill him?"

"I don't rightly know. It depends on what he does. But I can promise you this, ma'am . . . he won't ever bother you again."

"If you can . . . *kill him*!" The vehemence in her voice made Longarm's blood turn a little icy.

The next instant, he heard a footstep outside the door of the room, and he was already rolling off the young woman as the door opened and Clement stepped through. "It's nothing to worry about, darling," said Clement. "Everything is under control, and I have that champagne I promised you, to put you more in the mood—"

The light from the hallway fell through the open door and revealed Longarm standing beside the bed, the Colt in his hand leveled and cocked as he said wryly, "That's mighty kind of you, sweetheart, but there ain't enough champagne in the world to put me in mind of messing around with a skunk like you."

Clement didn't waste any breath exclaiming in surprise. He just flung the heavy glass bottle in his hand at Longarm's head and threw himself to the side as the lawman's gun roared.

Longarm tried to get out of the way of the champagne bottle, but fortune had guided Clement's throw. The bottle clipped Longarm on the side of the head, knocking his hat off and making bright red rockets explode behind his eyes. He was pretty sure his shot had missed. As he stumbled back a step toward the window, he saw the young woman go flying through the open door, and heard the slap of her bare feet as she fled down the corridor outside the bedroom. Knowing that she was clear, Longarm triggered the Colt twice more, firing blindly.

Clement crashed into him from the side, his hand clawing at the wrist of Longarm's gun hand. Both men went down, and Longarm's hand cracked against something hard, probably the edge of the bedside table. His fingers went numb, and the Colt slid out of them. Clement made a grab for the gun, but Longarm managed to twist around and kick it, sending the weapon skittering out of reach across the floor.

He had to end this fight in a hurry, Longarm knew. Those shots would bring the guard from downstairs, and he might summon more of Clement's men to come with him. Longarm planned to knock Clement out, recover his gun so that he could deal with the sentries, and haul Clement into the jungle with him. Then it would be just a matter of eluding the inevitable pursuit, reaching the port city with Clement as his prisoner, and taking him on board the ship that would ultimately carry them back to New Orleans.

That was all.

Longarm's right hand was still numb, so he used his left to punch Clement in the face as they rolled back and forth on the floor, grappling desperately with each other. Enough light came into the room from the hall for Longarm to be able to see what he was doing. Unfortunately, Clement was fighting like a madman, and even though Longarm was larger and heavier, the plantation owner held the advantage for the moment. Clement slammed his knee into Longarm's groin, and as agony shot through Longarm, making him double over, Clement managed to loop an arm around his throat from behind.

Clement's arm was like a bar of iron across Longarm's neck. Every time he turned around in this case, Longarm thought wildly, some son of a bitch was trying to strangle him. First it had been that blasted zombie, then one of Clement's men, and now Clement himself. Longarm was sick and tired of it.

He drove an elbow back into Clement's midsection. That loosened Clement's hold, and Longarm was able to grasp his arm and pull it away. As he twisted around, he gulped down

177

a breath of air to ease the terrible tightness in his chest and then clubbed both hands together and swung them at Clement's head. The blow sent Clement skidding away across the floor.

Longarm heard the rattle of gunfire close by, maybe as close as downstairs. He wasn't sure who was shooting at who, but for the time being, that didn't matter. He wanted to press his advantage over Clement, so he scrambled to his feet to lunge after the plantation owner.

Something rolled under Longarm's foot and dumped him hard on his back, knocking the breath out of him. That damn champagne bottle, he realized as he lay there half-stunned. It hadn't broken when it struck his head and then fell to the floor, and now it had tripped him up.

Worse than that, it rolled to a stop right beside Clement, who snatched it up and threw himself toward Longarm, holding the neck of the bottle with both hands as he raised it over his head.

That bottle was heavy enough to crush his skull when Clement brought it crashing down, Longarm knew. He gasped for air and gathered his muscles to try to get out of the way of the death blow.

He didn't have to make that probably futile effort because someone stepped into the room from the hallway, lifted a pistol, and squeezed off a shot. The bullet struck the bottle, shattering it and sending a shower of champagne and glass shards over both Longarm and Clement. Clement was left crouching over Longarm, the jagged bottle neck still clutched in his hands.

"Drop it, Clement," said Claudette, smoke curling up from the barrel of the revolver she held in her fist.

Longarm didn't know what was the most surprising: the sheer fact that Claudette was here, the lack of a Cajun accent in her voice as she spoke, the dark shirt and trousers she wore, so unlike anything he had seen her in before, or the accuracy with which her shot had broken the champagne bottle. All he could do was gape at her.

"Who . . . ?" gasped Clement.

"Call me Royale," said Claudette with a faint smile playing around her sensuous mouth.

With a scream of deranged hatred, Clement flipped the bottle neck around and plunged the jagged edge of the glass at Longarm's throat with the speed of a striking snake.

Claudette was faster. The gun in her hand boomed again, and Clement was thrown forward as the slug slammed into the back of his head, bored through his skull, and mushroomed out his forehead in a grisly shower of bone and brains. The bottle neck fell harmlessly to the floor as Clement pitched forward lifelessly. He flopped across Longarm's face, and Longarm hastily shoved the corpse aside in revulsion.

Claudette slid the gun into the black holster that was belted around her hips and came quickly across the room. "Are you all right, Custis?" she asked, still missing the Cajun accent.

"I'm fine," he said as he sat up and glanced at Clement's body with a grimace. "I never expected to see you here."

She knelt beside him. "I'm sorry I . . . had to deceive you."

"Outright lie to me, you mean." He chuckled grimly and shook his head. "Still, you just saved my life, so I reckon I can't get too riled up with you."

She helped him to his feet, and they walked out of the room without looking back at Clement's corpse. "Does that mean you're not going to arrest me?" she asked.

"When you've probably got a dozen or more men downstairs in the mood for trouble?"

"Closer to two dozen," she murmured. "I didn't know how well guarded Clement would be. I'm just sorry I didn't get here in time to save you the trouble of trying to get to him."

"You sailed out of New Orleans the same day I did, didn't you?" said Longarm.

"I have ships available to me," she said.

Longarm snorted. "I'll just bet you do. Smuggling ships."

179

"I never ran slaves, like Clement and Millard," she said tightly.

"No, but your men came damn close to killing me a few times. They *did* kill some of Millard's men."

She shrugged. "In war, men die. And it was war between Millard and me. I didn't know then that Clement was part of it. And I would have been willing to let things go on the way they had been if Millard's men hadn't ambushed a group of my couriers a few days before you arrived in New Orleans, Custis. They got the drop on my men, disarmed them . . . then shot them all in the back."

"Millard never mentioned *that* little detail when he said you were out to ruin him," Longarm said as they started down a broad, winding staircase to the first floor.

"Of course not. I never set out to hurt anybody, Custis. You have to believe that."

Longarm wasn't sure if he did or not, but at this point, it didn't really matter. He asked, "Why did you save me from your own men, down there in the shinneries?"

"I knew you were working with Millard. I thought I could use you to get close to him and find out his plans." Her hand reached over and stole into his. "But I didn't count on coming to feel about you the way I do now, Custis."

Longarm stopped and looked at her, and she leaned forward to kiss him. After a moment, his arms went around her, drawing her tightly to him. Then he broke the kiss and looked at her sadly. Her gaze dropped, and they started once more down the stairs, their hands no longer touching.

"You started the fire in the cane fields to draw Clement's guards away," Longarm said after a few seconds of silence between them. "Then you came here for Clement."

"I would have taken him prisoner and turned him over to you if I could have," she said quietly. "I really would have. He didn't give me any choice."

"No," said Longarm, "I reckon he didn't."

They crossed a luxuriously furnished drawing room and

went out through a foyer onto the veranda. Several men in derby hats stood outside the house, holding rifles. The body of the guard Clement had left on duty lay slumped on the ground nearby.

"Everything all right, ma'am?" asked one of the derby-hatted men.

"Yes," said Claudette. "Gather the workers we've freed tonight and take them back to the ship, Barry. We have room for them, don't we?"

"Yes, ma'am."

"Good. We'll take them back to New Orleans, or anywhere else they want to go."

The man nodded, and he and his companions moved off into the darkness.

"There's just one more thing I want to know," said Longarm.

"What's that?" asked Claudette.

"Why the masquerade as a bayou gal? Whose shack was that you took me to?"

"It was no masquerade," Claudette said softly. "That bayou girl was who I was, once upon a time . . . a long time ago. The shack belonged to my gran'pere, and everything I told you about him and his gran'mama and Marie Laveau was true."

"Too bad you had to reveal who you really are to your men."

"They already knew, no matter what Millard may have told you about the mysterious Royale. They're just loyal to me, that's all." She paused, then asked, "What happens now, Custis?"

Longarm looked into the distance, at the flames that were now dying out in the destroyed cane fields. "I've got no authority here," he said tonelessly. "In Saint Laurent, I'm just as much of an outlaw as you are. So I reckon you go your way and I go mine."

"Yes." She lifted a hand and touched his cheek lightly.

"But it is a pity that is the way it must be. If you and I were only on the same side . . ."

Still looking at the cane fields, Longarm said, "It's a pretty thing to think about, ain't it?"

Watch for

LONGARM AND THE BORDER WILDCAT

229th novel in the exciting LONGARM series
from Jove

Coming in January!

Explore the exciting Old West with one of the men who made it wild!